FIRST PLANE

Book Ten of the Hayle Coven Novels

PATTI LARSEN

Also by

PATTI LARSEN

Snow slid down the back of my jacket, but I didn't care. I was having too much fun swishing my arms and legs back and forth while my little sister, Meira, did the same beside me. The sound of her giggling warmed me up enough the bit of a cold trickle down my neck sneaking past the collar of my coat and knit scarf didn't bother me so much.

I squinted up into the bright sunlight as Liam bent over me, mittened hands on his knees, a huge smile on his face. Green glints danced in his hazel eyes, blonde hair sticking out from under his hat.

I accepted his hand and let him pull me to my feet, turning to observe my handiwork. A perfectly formed—if I do say so myself—snow angel imprinted the crisp white of the park behind town hall, joined by a second as Liam leaned in sideways and practically scooped Meira up from the ground. The floppy red pom-pom on the top of her multi-colored toque bobbed to one side as she cast a critical eye over what she'd made.

"Mine's cuter," she said, bumping me with her shoulder and covering her mouth with her mittens, eyes sparkling.

"Mine's bigger." I shoved her back, sticking out my tongue while I pulled free one of my gloves and warmed my nose with my bare hand. "Big trumps cute."

"I don't know." Liam looked back and forth between them. "Cute is pretty awesome."

She beamed at him and hugged him while he winked at me, just as a giant, shaggy, black dog bounded toward us, his fur caked with blobs of white, and dove head first to our feet, completely obliterating the two angels.

"Galleytrot!" Meira stomped one foot as the eager hound of the Wild Hunt panted a huge grin at us.

"Meira!" He ducked his nose into the snow, flinging some at her, to which she squealed. "I love snow!"

"Yeah, hadn't noticed." I found myself laughing while he rolled over and over, grunting as he rubbed his back on the cold ground, tail thrashing, eyes flickering with red fire.

I turned to Liam, one hand in my jacket pocket. Yes. It was still there. My little gift, nice and safe, waiting for me to deliver it. Just as my fingers closed around it, Liam turned to me with a smile, bending over me, his handsome face pink from the cold.

Before I could do or say anything, he hugged me, pressing

his cheek into my hair. I pulled free my gift, hugging him back, though I could feel my skin heat as Meira giggled again, a wicked look in her eyes, blue flashing to amber as she watched us.

I caught a glimpse of Charlotte over his shoulder, also watching, but my wereguard's normal flat expression told me nothing. Surprise, surprise. I'd been getting better at reading her lately, but I was already flustered enough having my little sister watch Liam hug me.

Don't get me wrong, he gave great hugs. But there was the little thing about him and his feelings for me while I, the idiot—yes, I admitted it—still couldn't bring myself to completely let go of Quaid. He'd dumped me, his choice, left me for the Enforcers and freedom, not wanting to be tied to a coven leader. But my heart, despite my resolve to let him go, didn't want to just yet.

And it was nowhere near fair to Liam to begin a relationship with him until it did.

Which meant we were friends, though the farce was hard to maintain at times, my guilt occasionally getting the better of me. Yet here I was, accepting his affection as usual.

At least I had something for him to break the mood.

Boy, would it.

I slid my arms around his neck and dumped the perfectly

formed snowball I'd been saving for him down the back of his shirt.

Cruel? Oh yeah. Funny? You freaking betcha.

Liam did the snow dance, laughing and howling all at the same time, jerking his shirt out of his pants under his bulky jacket, shaking it and himself until Meira and I were senseless in convulsive laughter. Even Charlotte smiled a little while Galleytrot snorted and shook his big head, snow pattering from his fur.

Liam turned at last, panting and flushed, eyes slits as he focused on me.

"You did *not*." It made me laugh harder when he used one of my favorite expressions.

"I so *did*." I crossed my arms over my chest and smirked. "Come on then, Sidhe. Let's see what you've got."

Snowball fights rock. Especially when I win.

Finally worn out and ready to go inside for some hot chocolate, Meira, Charlotte and I left Liam and Galleytrot behind, the pair retreating with happy waves into town hall and the Sidhe cavern housing the Gate Liam guarded. My invite for them to join us was sweetly turned down, Liam eager to go back to his studying.

That boy. He needed to get his head out of books more often.

Thus the impromptu snow party. As we trudged back, I found myself smiling at the Christmas decorations gracing each house, the white lights wrapping each evergreen the town erected waiting for dark so they could begin their twinkling show. I was happy to be home for break. As much as I really liked school and was having a great time now that the Star Club and their tainted connection to Ameline finally disbanded, I missed being home.

There hadn't been any news from the former Dumont heir. I hadn't forgotten about her—hard to do when she almost killed me twice—but I had allowed Mom to lull me into a bit of a less paranoid state when she claimed she and the High Council weren't dropping the ball. Now leader of that Council, Mom had multiple Enforcers out looking for Ameline and I knew my mother was as determined as I to find the girl and bring her to justice.

The nice part was, even though things had been strained between Mom and I since the whole Ameline incident at the first of the semester, we'd both softened and let most of our animosity go. Okay, not all of it. But enough we weren't snarking at each other every five seconds. And despite being super busy with her new duties and unavailable most of the time, Mom promised this Christmas week she'd be ours one hundred percent. No Council business.

Yeah, I'd believe that when it happened. Still, the alternative to having a mother as Council Leader wasn't pretty. Namely, the whole of witchdom forced to watch her burned at the stake for allowing Dad to use blood magic in our house rather than taking the leader's seat on the Council.

I guess I could handle her being busy.

"Do you think Mom will like her present?" Meira was ten already, amazing. And growing like a weed. She stood to my shoulder and looked much more mature than most kids her age. The last six months had seen her demon features changing, as though she'd reached some milestone Demonicon marked, but we didn't know about. It freaked me out a bit to see my little sister look like she was going on fourteen when she was still so young to me, but there wasn't much I could do about it. When she reached out with one hand and took mine, smiling like the little kid I held in my heart, I still felt the girl inside her and that made it okay.

"I know she will." We didn't necessarily celebrate Christmas, per se. Not the religious form of it, anyway. But it had been a tradition in our family for as long as I could remember, Mom's attempt to make Meira and I feel like we were more like normal people, so present buying and stocking stuffing were still big parts of our celebration.

"Maybe we should get the other one." I smiled as Meira fretted over the pentagram necklace we'd chosen for Mom. She'd lost her favorite one over the summer and no amount of searching magic uncovered it. I knew it meant a lot to her, but it was Meira who suggested replacing it. We'd combed all the stores in Boston, finally narrowing our choices down to two.

"I like the one with the diamonds in it," I said. "You did too."

Meira bobbed a nod. "I know," she said. "But the other one was more traditional."

"We could have just made one, you know." I found myself laughing at her.

"I know," Meira said. "I just didn't think we could get it right."

Agreed. Neither of us was very good with metal yet. "We made the right choice. Those five diamonds were perfect to hold the different element fragments we embedded."

Meira grinned at me. "You're right," she sighed happily. "Now she can carry a bit of each of us around with her all the time." We'd both contributed a sliver of power, one for each gem.

"It was a great idea," I hugged her to me as we walked. "You're very thoughtful."

Her smile broadened before she startled me with her next question.

"Are you and Liam dating?"

Choke. "Um…"

She shrugged like it was no big deal. "I really like him," she said while Charlotte coughed softly behind me. Translation: Charlotte was laughing her fool noggin off inside her head.

Sigh.

Before I could offer my sister some clever answer that wouldn't answer her question one way or the other, we both tensed. Not for a bad reason, for once. Meira's little grin grew into wide-eyed excitement as she hopped up and down in the snow.

The rush of demon magic filled me with warmth as Dad crossed over.

Girls, he sent, rich mental voice touching us both. *I'm home.*

I grabbed Meira's hand, feeling Charlotte rush forward to my side as I turned to her. "The veil."

She nodded quickly and took my other before I pulled open the barrier between planes and rode it home. I loved the freedom of riding the veil between planes, the rubbery surface welcoming me as always. Not only was it fun and exhilarating, it meant we were saved running for five minutes through slush, instead dumped a heartbeat later into our very toasty kitchen and Dad's arms.

Not a moment to waste. At least Mom had brought his effigy home with her from Harvard for the holidays instead of leaving him alone there. He used to visit more often, now that he had his new and improved diamond statue to feed him energy. But those frequent trips from Demonicon to us had tapered off again. I could only guess he was busy because of his responsibilities as a Demon Prince of the Second Plane, a promotion he'd acquired since Sassy, my demon cat sans demon boy, almost died to give Dad the power to cross over after his original effigy was destroyed.

Long story. Complicated. Like most of my life.

Meira got to hug Dad first, but I didn't begrudge her the chance. Not while Mom and my grandmother exchanged worried glances before both staring at me like they knew something that wasn't going to make me very happy.

Lovely. What now? I'd spent the last two years or so staggering from one ginormous disaster to another. I was kind of liking the quiet, thanks. But there was no hint of trepidation in Dad's expression when he finally released Meira and opened his arms to me.

I don't care how old I grew or what I went through, there was nothing that could make me feel better than a hug from my father. He was tall, strong and hummed with power, which made my demon very happy.

"Hey, Dad." I looked up at him with a smile. "Nice to see you."

"Hi, cupcake." Jeeze, would he ever drop that stupid nickname? I was eighteen, for goodness sakes. But the sparkle in his blue eyes, his human disguise in place hiding the true amber of his gaze, told me he would never, ever stop.

Sigh.

It wasn't until Dad let me go, one hand still on my

shoulder, the other reaching out to ruffle Meira's hair now her funny hat was discarded, I turned back to Mom and Gram and fixed them both with a stare of my own.

"What's up?" I tipped my head to the side, catching sight of Sassafras perched on the table just behind Mom's elbow, as if he were hiding. From what?

Dad's hand tightened while Mom spoke. "Your father has some news."

Gram snorted. "Is that what you call it?" Ethpeal Hayle spent seventeen years of her adult life fading in and out of reality. Now that she was whole again—or as whole as she would ever be—she didn't even try to temper her sharp tongue. "I call it a really bad idea."

No matter how crazy Gram was, then and now, I trusted her instincts. If she was against whatever was coming, it couldn't be good. I turned on Dad while Mom clenched her hands together in the lap of her black velvet skirt, forehead pinched together, aging her. When had Mom started getting wrinkles? I would have blamed the Council and all the weight of her duties, but I was sure I'd given her most of them myself.

"Your grandmother." Dad paused while both of us, my sister and I, glanced at Gram. "No, girls," he said, voice gentle. "Your other grandmother."

Oh. Um. Wow. "Yeah?" It didn't come out the most intelligently, but I managed while Meira stared at him with her mouth hanging open.

"I've done my best to hold her off," he said. "But she insists on meeting you."

"Not going to happen." "Harry, this is a terrible idea."

Mom and Gram agreeing? Oh boy. But this time I was the one on the outside of the two of them.

And I wasn't alone.

"What's she like?" Meira's surprise was replaced by a little smile. "I really want to meet her, Dad."

"So do I." And had since my last trip to Demonicon, searching for the means to save Dad, only to discover he had a vast family on the other plane I'd never even known or thought about.

"It's just for dinner." Dad sounded almost apologetic as he focused on Mom and Gram. "I'll have them back in no time."

Gram snorted. "This is stupid," she snapped. "Risky and stupid. The girl's a coven leader, Harry. She can't just run off to another plane like this. Not when we have no idea what kind of danger this puts her in."

Danger? And hang on a minute, I wasn't the only one going. Why no concern about Meira? I reached for my sister's hand. "Should we be worried?"

Dad shook his head, scowling at Gram a moment while Mom's agitation grew. I could tell she wanted to say something, but also knew she was very loyal to Dad and was probably hesitating to speak against him.

"There's no danger," Dad said. "We're just going to dinner."

Sassafras grunted as he moved to the edge of the table and sat again, thick tail wrapping around his paws like a furry stole. "You can't guarantee that," he said. "Which is why, if you insist on taking the girls, I'm coming with you."

Mom looked relieved, even reaching out to stroke his fur, but Gram's face twisted into a scowl.

"That's a comfort, fur ball," she said.

"Oh hush, you crazy old bat." He flicked his ears at her. "I know what I'm doing."

"So it's settled." I smiled up at Dad, feeling suddenly excited about the proposition. I'd liked Demonicon, or at least the sliver of it I'd been able to see when I was there. How everything was magic and the city itself hummed with power. I grinned down at Meira. "When do we go?"

"Not until tomorrow," Dad said. "I don't want to risk being there after dark. So we'll leave at lunch. I'll have you back in plenty of time."

Right. The legend thing I'd been warned about the first

time I went to Demonicon said we could be trapped there if we stayed after dark. No one even knew if it was true or not. I let the worry drop and focused on the fun.

Demonicon. My grandmother. Probably uncles, aunts, cousins.

How cool was that?

"Excuse me." Charlotte's voice shook a little. I turned to her, startled. She had a way of surprising me, so quiet, always around, but so good at her job as wereguard I didn't know she was there half the time despite my attempts to make her just be my friend. "You're leaving?"

"Dad's plane." I waited while her flawless face crumpled a little.

"I'm coming with you." It wasn't a question.

"You can't." I glanced at Dad who shook his head. "You have to be a demon."

Charlotte's skin paled to the point I worried she might pass out. "I have to come with you."

Not for the first time I wondered if the bond between me and my bodywere was linked with magic. Her sudden strong reaction pretty much confirmed my suspicions, though I'd never thought to check and see if there was a magic connection between us.

"It'll be fine," I told her, leaving Dad so I could comfort

Charlotte as she shook a little. "I'll only be gone a couple of hours."

Her blonde hair swung as she shook her head. "You can't leave me." Her whisper came out hoarse and broken.

"There, you see?" Gram sat back, arms crossed over her chest. "Syd can't go. End of this ridiculous plan."

I spun on Gram with a scowl. "It's my decision," I said with more heat than I intended.

"Your coven comes first." She shot it back at me like we were firing missiles at each other. It surprised me, since Gram usually had my back.

"I'm going." I nodded to Dad who looked sad, but nodded too. I returned my attention to Charlotte. "You'll be fine."

She visibly took a hold of herself and grunted softly in answer.

Man, was I going to pay for leaving her behind.

Dad didn't stay long, promising to come back for us, while he and Mom retreated to the basement. Gram huffed off, her fluffy dressing gown drawn tight around her thin body, flashy striped socks silent on the floor, just how she liked it.

Meira ran off to her room to change while Charlotte sat, stone faced and gaze locked on anything but me. I left her in the kitchen, Sassafras trailing behind me as I retreated to my own room for a moment to think.

Surprisingly, my chubby silver Persian didn't come in with me, but kept sashaying his way down the hall to Meira's door. I felt a little abandoned, but then again some privacy would be nice.

I was just stripping off my t-shirt, my black cotton bra strap about to be unhooked when a familiar power touched my mind.

Syd.

Why was I blushing? Quaid couldn't see me standing there half-undressed. And it wasn't not like he hadn't seen the full show, not after we'd spent a night together last fall.

With mixed emotions, a jumble of nerves, frustration, love and anger all piled together, I walled off what I was feeling and let him touch me. Normally he would have been with me all the time, but when he rejected me, my demon severed the magical connection we had and I'd missed the feeling of him ever since. Sure, I still had the family magic to hold him to me, but it wasn't the same as the intimate thread of magic we'd shared.

Quaid. Cool, calm, collected. Yay me. *How are you?* We hadn't had much contact at school. He was too busy ignoring me in favor of his stupid Enforcer trainee friends.

I wasn't bitter.

He paused. *I'm okay*, he sent, tentative. Damn, was I broadcasting? But no, my shield was firmly in place.

Maybe that was the problem. I'd never really tried to hide anything from him before. But could he blame me for being cautious?

Where are you? He'd vanished from campus the day before I headed home for the holidays and I realized I had no idea where he would go. Could go. His only family was his sister Mia, the Dumont coven leader and she was pretty messed up, hands full with a decaying coven caving in on its own evil. And the kind couple who'd taken him in, Martin and Louisa Vega, members of my coven, were dead, murdered during Mom's trial in the spring.

Nowhere. He sounded tired. Sad. Naturally, my heart opened. *Sorry to bother you. I'm just checking in to make sure you're okay.*

He hadn't cared all semester. And yet, I'd seen enough of him… was he keeping tabs on me? Despite our breakup and the choice he made to leave me, it made me wonder if he still loved me.

Bad Syd. No going there.

Everyone has gone home, he sent. *I'm just trying to figure out what to do for the holidays.*

Ah. Now we were getting somewhere. My annoyance

returned. So I was default girl, huh? Now that honey-blonde with the big rack was with her folks for Christmas, all of a sudden good old Syd was looking better.

Jerkorama.

And yet, I couldn't bring myself to be cruel. He'd spent his whole life alone, with adopted parents who used him for a power source, only to discover they'd murdered his real family. Quaid had never really belonged, not even with the Dumonts. Thankfully not with the Dumonts. The only place he'd really ever found a home was with our coven.

Why don't you come to Wilding Springs for Christmas? The offer was out of me and winging its way before I could stop myself.

Quaid hesitated again, but this time when I spoke up, I tapped into the family magic, feeling better about the idea the more I thought it through.

The Hayles are still your family, I sent. *You're still tied to our magic until you take your Enforcer vows. You're very welcome here, Quaid.*

Spoken like a true coven leader.

I wondered, had I spoken as myself, as the girl who wanted all of a sudden to hug him and kiss him and feel his delicious power wrap me up, would the outcome have been different?

I felt his rejection the moment he decided. *Thank you, but no.* Two could play at the tough guy routine, it turned out. *I'm going to check in on Mia. Might spend time with her, if I can stand it.*

How is she? I hadn't had contact with Mia since the night Ameline attacked, taking Rupert, who I knew as Blood and Mia's last connection to the girl she thought she was, away as her slave. Mia spiraled down into depression, disappearing from school and making it quite clear she wanted to be left alone.

Since we were both coven leaders, if I pushed her on the issue it could be construed as interference. I had to back down.

She's not great, he sent, guilt in his tone. Was he regretting not being there for her, for going on with his own life? A secret, cruel part of me hoped so. *I'm worried about her.*

I couldn't go there. Even talking to Quaid about it might get me in trouble. *Well, say hi for me*, I sent. *And the offer is open.*

That was better. A little less bossy, a little more me. Quaid hugged me gently with his power.

I might take you up on that, he sent softly.

Just wait until after tomorrow. I shook my head as

I thought. *I won't be around until after that and I'd really like to see you.*

Where are you going? His curiosity perked, almost visible through our connection.

I filled him in quickly, trying not to come across too excited, but it was harder to hide my enthusiasm than it had been my other emotions.

Is Ethpeal right? Quaid's concern touched me like a heated thread through his magic. *Is it dangerous?*

I thought about it a moment. *I don't see how*, I sent. *We'll be with Dad, going to the most secure building on Demonicon, the royal palace. Unless there's some civil unrest he's failed to tell us about—and trust me, Dad wouldn't—the only real concern is getting us home before dark so we don't test the whole legend thingie.*

Okay, he sent. *Just be careful. And watch your back.*

I will. I paused a moment, so many things I wanted to tell him welling inside me, but knowing I couldn't go there. He'd made his choice.

And from the sadness in his tone, he was struggling too. *I might see you.*

I hope so.

His power hugged me again before he left me and I spent a long time sitting on the edge of my bed with a fresh t-shirt in my hands, unable to focus enough to put it on, my heart full of Quaid all over again.

Damn him.

I have no idea what I was thinking as I finally pulled myself together enough to finish dressing. All I knew was my temper was rising and I needed to vent.

How dare Quaid reach for me after all this time, be nice, sweet even, worry about me? Treat me like there might still be something between us, *hug* me for goodness sakes? Twice? I wanted to be mad, to rage to someone about his absolute arrogance and could only think of one person who would listen to me in this shape.

Liam came right to the entry of the cavern as I stormed my way through the shields and he just stood there, his mouth open a little, eyes wide as I dove right into what became a ten-minute rant about Quaid and what a jerk he was.

"… arrogant, bossy, over bearing, how dare he think he can just contact me and everything's all freaking okay and crap? Because it's not okay, not even a little bit, him and his high and mighty jerkathonabration of three whole months being a total ass not even giving me the time of day, flaunting around with those Enforcer friends of his. Who aren't, by the way. Trainees. Yeah. *Trainees* who think everyone around them should give a rat's furry behind. Jerkwads in training more like."

Not like Liam hadn't heard this particular performance before. Every slight, imagined or otherwise, Liam was my go-to guy. He listened with sympathy, agreed with me Quaid was an absolute ass who didn't deserve to breathe the same air as me and held me when my typical raving wound down into a tear-soaked sob fest.

But when I spun to fire off another nasty line, I saw the hurt and anger in Liam's face, sharp enough it brought me to an abrupt halt.

"What?" I held up both hands while Charlotte sat down on the floor next to Galleytrot and gave his big head a good scratch, face expressionless even as the black dog's eyes flared with red fire.

"Nothing." Liam walked into the library section of the chamber, turning his back to me as he rifled through parchment and quills on his desk. I grabbed his arm and spun him around to face me. Only to wince at the pain on his face.

"Something," I said. "Liam."

He shrugged, a rather violent gesture for someone normally so sweet and kind. "I'm just getting tired of it, that's all."

"Tired of what?" I'm not normally clueless, but where was the problem? Not like we hadn't been here before.

Awareness dawned. Syd, you idiot.

"You know how I feel about you." Liam wouldn't meet my eyes, head down, voice quiet, the rumble of it rough with emotion as he confirmed what my very selfish brain just realized. "And you know I don't care you don't feel the same." He finally looked up, hazel eyes rimmed with moisture. "But when you talk about him all the time…"

I lurched forward and hugged Liam, pressing my nose into his chest, breathing in the scent of rich earth and fabric softener, feeling his arms around me and kicking myself mentally for hurting the only person who never, ever, hurt me back.

"I'm sorry," I whispered. "Liam, I'm such a jerk."

"No," he said. "You're not." He drew a deep breath, gently pushed me away. Even managed a little smile, bless him. "I'm here for you, no matter what. You can talk to me about anything. Even him."

I shook my head. "No more," I said. "I can't believe you put up with me for this long. Besides, he made his choice.

I just don't know how to get him out of here." I thumped one fist against my chest, where my heart pounded painfully once before settling again. "I really want him out."

Liam didn't say anything for a moment, but when he finally spoke, there was so much love in his voice I wanted to cry.

"No, you don't," he said. "But that's okay."

I opened my mouth to protest—was it false protest?—only to have Liam take my hand and smile for real.

"I know you don't love me the way I love you," he said with the same simple, kind, quietness I adored about him. "That you don't feel for me what you do for Quaid. It's my own fault for not doing everything I can to let you go. But I can't help it either. And no matter how much it might hurt at times, I don't want you out of here either." He pressed my captured hand to his chest, the beating of his pulse heavy under my palm.

I was the most horrible person who ever lived.

Before I could implode from my sheer terribleness, I filled Liam in on the trip to Demonicon, at the very least to change the subject.

"Just be careful," he said as he guided me to the exit, Charlotte drifting out into the basement alone to check ahead. Why did everyone keep saying that to me? They were making me nervous. "But have fun, too. I can't wait to hear what happens."

There, see? The perfect guy, really. Equal parts support and concern.

What the hell was wrong with me I couldn't feel the same about Liam as he felt for me?

After another gentle hug, I slipped through the portal and headed for the main floor. But the sound of claws clicking on stone and the huff of hot breath on my hand made me pause. I turned and found Galleytrot on my heels, looking up at me.

"We need to talk," he said.

Nothing good ever followed those words.

"Okay." I waved Charlotte off and trailed after the big hound into one of the storage rooms. I knew she'd hover outside and hear everything we said, but the one thing I'd learned about Charlotte was she knew how to keep her mouth shut.

Galleytrot sank to his haunches, fixing me with his endlessly deep black eyes. "I'm worried about Liam."

A shot of panic raced through me. "Is he okay?" If anything happened to him, we'd be in so much trouble. He was the last of the O'Danes, the only one who could answer the knock of the Sidhe when it came once a year.

Without him, the Gate would open and the Seelie and Unseelie would pour into our world again.

"It's not physical." Galleytrot chuffed softly. "It's an affliction of the heart."

I pulled back. Wasn't I feeling badly enough already the big mutt had to bring it up?

"None of your business," I said. Actually, half snapped, half mumbled.

"It is my business," he said. "The health and wellbeing of the Gatekeeper is very important to me." He sighed out a breath. "To all of us."

"I know," I whispered. "I can't help it."

The dog nodded slowly. "I'm not asking you to change your heart's desire," he said. "No one can do that. And trying can be disastrous." He leaned forward and licked my hand. "I just want you to promise me you won't break his heart."

That was the last thing I wanted, too. So I nodded and watched as Galleytrot left me, padding his enormous way through the door and back across the hall, disappearing in a flash of Sidhe green magic.

If only I could assure myself I could keep my promise, we'd be all set.

I took the slow way home, choosing to huddle inside my jacket in the dark, the sparkling lights of the corner trees doing little to elevate my mood. I could have simply rode the veil home again, but like my stomping trip to town hall, I needed the drawn-out foot dragging on my way back just as much.

My boot caught a clump of snow, now brown from the many car tires splashing old dirt and salt from the roadway to coat the sidewalk in ugly slush. Kind of ruined the pretty, pristine whiteness I loved.

No metaphors there or anything.

The house was quiet when I walked in, cheeks cold and hands stuffed in my pockets since I'd forgotten my gloves when I stormed out earlier. I still felt Dad downstairs, but knew I'd be spending lots of time with him in the very near future and decided to let Mom have his sole company for the evening.

Besides, they didn't need my mood dragging them down.

I'd made a promise to myself not to wallow, not to doubt myself anymore, and for the most part I was doing a good job upholding that promise. But, other times I found it really hard not to sink into my old patterns of poor me and just curl up in bed with a bag of chips and a really cheesy romance novel I could blubber over.

Instead, I slipped into my favorite yoga pants and t-shirt and sat at my desk to check my email. Among the spam offering me sexual enhancement aids and Nigerian princes asking me to rescue them, I found myself grinning at several welcomed emails.

The first was from Tippy Meeks, the well-endowed redhead I'd made friends with thanks to my college roomie, Sashenka Hensley. Her rambling emails were familiar to me, as she went on and on about which boys in her coven she had a total hunger for, how she ruined her favorite pair of heels and all about the after-Christmas shopping she was dying to do. It was enough of a distraction I was giggling at her very naughty description of the guy who lived next door to her who had the habit of leaving his curtains open if she did the same.

Oh my flaming cheeks.

The next one was from Mia, short and sweet, wishing me a happy holiday. Nothing personal, not a mention she even wrote it, one coven leader courtesy to another. It broke my heart and I fired off an answer in the same language to her just so she could keep up whatever appearances she felt she had to.

Third was from Tallah, our usual political/coven conversation continuation. I adored the leader of the Hensley coven as much as her sister, valued her outlook on the world and her insights into the future of witches once younger generations had control of the covens. There were three of the big six now in the hands of new leaders— if we could count Mia's disastrous attempts to rein in the Dumonts—so we were on a much more even keel when it came to addressing issues at Council.

Not that I was ever invited to do anything about issues at Council. Erica Plower, Mom's former second and the very person I assigned to take the Hayle coven seat, had a bad habit of treating me like her daughter too, only handing out information as she thought I needed it.

I didn't push things, partly because Gram was my co-leader and I trusted her not to let Erica run roughshod over the pair of us. Not that I didn't think Erica had our best interests at heart, but she was Mom's best friend and her allegiance was to the Council now.

The final one I saved for last, happily clicking on Sashenka's message.

I thought Mia's was short and sweet.

Skype when you're home?

I checked and found her online, immediately calling for a face-to-face.

When she answered, I beamed at her, almost bouncing in my chair I was so happy to see her. We'd gotten off to a rocky start the first of the semester, but since she let go of her need to try to impress me and the pressure her coven leader sister put on her to excel, Sashenka actually turned into a bit of a wild girl and dragged me along with her.

"Syd!" She waved with enthusiasm, her room bright behind her. She lived in California, four long hours behind me, and the sun still shone in her bedroom window, the ocean just visible on the horizon through her softly undulating curtains.

"Hey, Shenka." I rested my chin on my fists. "Man, it looks really nice there."

She glanced back over her shoulder. "Yeah, just got back from surfing." She tossed her long, black hair over her shoulder, still wet from her swim. "You have to come visit this summer. We'll have a blast."

"Done." I let out a long sigh, not meaning to, but the relief of talking to someone who knew me really well tapped into my emotions.

"Uh-oh." Her expression fell, concern all over her pretty face, dark eyes fixed on me. "You okay?"

I nodded quickly. "Yeah, fine," I said. "You put up with me dumping on you all semester. I'm not doing it now. Besides, it's nothing you haven't heard before."

Sashenka's lower lip popped out at she nodded in sympathy. "Quaid."

"And Liam." I sat back and grinned at her, though I felt like a total idiot. "Why did you let me drop all that Quaid stuff on the guy who thinks he's in love with me?"

She snorted softly, rolling her eyes, white teeth flashing against her dark skin. "Like you would have listened to me," she said. "Besides, Liam is a great shoulder." She paused. "Two shoulders, actually."

Go away, stab of jealousy. Sashenka meant her compliment in the best way.

"I know," I said. "He kind of gave it to me tonight. Finally told me he was tired of it." I let her see my guilt. "I feel terrible. Why didn't I ever think of his feelings? I'm such a jerk."

Sashenka didn't say anything for a long moment, so long I was starting to feel sorry for myself after all, despite my choice otherwise.

"It's really hard to see what's right in front of us

sometimes," she finally said, voice thoughtful. "How the one we want is bad for us, but the one we need is so familiar and there all the time we don't even realize what could happen if we just let go of one and embrace the other." She flushed, pink rising to shine in her dark cheeks. "That came out stupid."

"No," I said, "it didn't." She was so right it made me want to shake myself. "You're saying I only want Quaid because I can't have him, but I don't want Liam because I can?"

Damn it. I hated psychology. Especially when the twinge in my gut said there might be something to it.

Sashenka's smile was gentle. "Just something to think about, maybe? You've been struggling with this for a while—it might be time to ask yourself why."

Like I didn't have enough to think about. I quickly filled her in on my pending visit to Dad's plane and got the same warning and concern mixed with partial excitement from her I had from Liam.

I was ready to sign off, climb into bed and try to get a good night's sleep when Sashenka stopped me.

"Syd," she said, hesitant, face scrunched as though she struggled with what she was about to say.

"Just say it," I said with a smile. "I won't take it the wrong way. I promise."

She nodded quickly and sighed. "I'm jealous," she said. "Of you and Liam. Of how much he loves you. I just wish you'd see it, too."

She hung up the video call before I could answer.

It was a long time before my churning thoughts let me finally fall asleep.

I had just set one stumbling foot on the floor at the bottom of the stairs, rubbing sleepily at my face after a night of tossing and turning, when my progress was suddenly blocked by a very cranky old lady. Gram grasped the railing with one hand, putting herself in my way so I had to stop and take what she was about to dish out.

"Listen to me, girl," she said, voice almost a hiss as her blue eyes trapped me with their intensity, no longer the faded color I was used to, but flooded with magic. "If you let anything happen to yourself over there, I'm bringing you back from the dead and kicking your skinny ass."

Her whole body shook, lips turned down into a frown so deep her mouth almost disappeared completely in the folds of her wrinkles. I'd never seen her so upset.

No, not upset.

Afraid.

I reached out and hugged her, pulling her resisting and

stiffened body against me, feeling the boniness of her through her pink fluffy housecoat, how she trembled, a relentless statue of anxiety.

Gram, I sent. *I love you.*

If I'd wondered why she'd not touched my mind to deliver her message, something much more common than her actually opening her mouth to speak, I understood the moment my thoughts reached hers.

Gram's body crumpled into mine as she finally clung to me, her heart wide open, the terror and frustration she felt raw and anguished.

I love you too, Sydlynn Thaddea Hayle. Her mental voice shook as much as her frail body. *Don't you ever leave me.*

I pulled back and tried to smile, though it was hard through the tears choking me, the tightness in my throat threatening my air supply. I cleared it twice before I could speak out loud.

"You really need to learn to trust me."

Gram's tension eased slightly as she blew a raspberry with her thin lips. "Trust you? You, I trust." She pinched my arm so hard I let out a yelp and covered the offended area with my other hand. "That demon bitch? Never."

Okay then. And while I couldn't bring myself to chalk Gram's attitude up to jealousy, I wondered at her attitude.

"Something I should know about what's happening here?" I was done playing. Time for answers.

Gram crossed her arms over her chest, tried for stern crazy lady with a heart of stone. I knew better.

"Just watch yourself." She shook her head, white fluff of her hair swaying as she did. "I don't like her or her politics. Hell, Harry doesn't like her and she's his mother." Gram softened, fingers stroking over my cheek. "Just be careful. Promise me."

"I promise." There the warning was again. Like I was running off to do something stupid. But now she had me really worried. There had been times in the past a good dose of worry actually saved my butt, so I wasn't really complaining, but it definitely took the fun out of my anticipation.

Gram turned and stumped her way back down the hall, going into her room and thudding the door shut solidly behind her. I wouldn't call it slamming, exactly, but she was pretty close.

Okay then.

Things were forcefully lighthearted in the kitchen as Mom served up pancakes with her false smile telling me loud and clear she just wanted everything to be okay. There was a time I almost bought her act, mostly because I didn't want to know otherwise. But the older I became, the more experience I had, the easier it was to see right through her.

I hugged her around the spatula and bowl of batter in her hands, letting my magic out to her for the first time in a long time. Her power embraced mine swiftly, almost desperately, as though she'd been waiting for me to make the first move.

Mom, I sent. *I love you, you know. It's going to be okay.*

Oh, Syd. Her power held me as much as her arms did. *We have so much to talk about.*

I pulled back, met her eyes. *Like?*

I've been a terrible mother. Her face crumpled a little, but she still clung to her smile, more for her own sake I was thinking than Meira's or mine. *These past few months have been hard on you and your sister. And I haven't been there for you the way I've wanted to.*

All the resentment and bitterness washed away as she smiled at me, really smiled, and when she pulled free her magic remained with me as she dished out another batch of pancakes.

We spent the morning talking about everything from school to politics to the newest batch of dancers on my favorite competition show, sitting in the living room, curled up on the sofa in our pajamas, the three of us laughing and sharing like we used to when I was young. Gram even joined us, her smartass comments mixed with Sassy's dry humor filling me up with so much love for my family I almost reconsidered going with Dad.

Meira finally left to get ready, but I lingered, watching Gram totter off, Sassy swaying his fat cat way behind her. Before I could leave, Mom reached out to me again.

Quaid. She said his name in my head paired with a rush of love and protection drawing out sobs threatening to crush my chest. *I know he hurt you. I wanted to be there for you. But I wasn't.*

Mom. I could only get that one word out before I crumpled sideways, my head in her lap, and cried over my still-broken heart. I told her everything, how I'd given him all of me and it just wasn't enough. She didn't judge, didn't get upset, just stroked my hair and let me feel how much she loved me.

This was what I needed, what I'd craved since Quaid broke up with me months earlier, after I'd been foolish enough to surrender my body, heart and soul to him. I just needed my mother to tell me everything was going to be okay. Weird how I held onto it for so long.

I finally sat up as Mom leaned close and stroked my hair away from my tear-stained cheeks. "It is, you know," she whispered. "Going to be all right. But you and Quaid have a destiny, my beautiful, powerful, amazing child. Whatever that destiny turns out to mean for you both, I don't know. Only that I'm here for you, always. Always."

I hugged her and nodded into her hair, heart the lightest it had been in months. "Thanks, Mom."

She sighed softly and kissed my cheek before letting me go. "Now," she said. "Promise me something."

"Let me guess." I rolled my eyes, but grinned as I swiped at the wetness on my face with the hem of my t-shirt. "Be careful on Demonicon."

Mom's little smile back was brief as fear flashed in her eyes. "You are perfectly capable of taking care of yourself," she said, shocking me right to the tips of my toes. Really? She thought that? "But I'm your mother. And I worry. You and your sister are very important to me, you know, no matter how things have been between us lately."

"I know," I said. "I can live with that." A tiny flutter of my own fear raced through me. "Is she really so bad?" Dad didn't talk about his family at all. In fact, I'd never really even thought about how he had to have parents, siblings, cousins. Not until Sassy's father, Theridialis, mentioned them to me when I was on Demonicon, trying to save Dad.

What was I walking into?

"Your grandmother is… a powerful demon." Mom's hands tightened into fists in her lap. "She has been Ruler for so long, it's all she knows. And that affects her choices. Her actions."

Did Mom worry she might be falling under the same influence? Maybe. But if so, she didn't confess it to me.

"Look after your sister." She patted my hand and rose to her feet, as tall and elegant as always, though the sunlight streaming through the window highlighted the deepening lines in her once flawless face and the strand or two of silver now running through her midnight hair. "And whatever happens, come home before dark."

"We will," I said.

I spent a reflective half hour in the shower, thinking about Quaid, Mom, Gram, my sister. About Liam and Sashenka and my dad. The trip I was about to take. And even though it should have left me swirling with confusion and mentally worn out, I found myself refreshed, almost light-hearted, when I emerged from the steam and hot water.

Maybe I was growing up finally.

I chose my clothing carefully, slipping into a nice blue sundress, my best color, and cute silver shoes, even wearing the lovely pentagram necklace Mom gave me for my fifteenth birthday, a match to the one she'd always worn.

I stared at it as I stood in front of the mirror, realizing I'd never actually had it on my body. How had I not sensed the thread of Mom's magic running through it, the touch of her present in it? No wonder I'd rejected it back then when I didn't want anything to do with magic. But it reminded me of the one Meira and I replaced, and as I held the shining silver in my palm, I promised myself I'd never again take it off.

With my simple layer of mascara, lip gloss and my mother's power to fortify me, I descended to the kitchen, reaching the bottom of the stairs just as I felt Dad's power flood the basement.

He emerged in the sunlit kitchen as I entered, hugging Mom who looked like she was doing her best not to cry. Gram was nowhere in sight and when I tried to reach her with my magic she cut me off.

Her leave me alone sign was hung and I wasn't about to push her.

Mom followed us down the stairs, Sassy scampering first as Dad let Meira and I go ahead of him. I glanced over my shoulder at Charlotte who padded silently behind me, head down, face pale.

The familiar tingle of family magic ran into my feet and up my legs as I stepped onto the concrete floor and approached the pentagram. Before Mom could ask, I reached out to the coven, my coven, and let them feel me with them.

Meira and I have been invited to meet my grandmother on Demonicon. I'd thought long and hard about what to tell them and decided straight forward was the way to go. *We'll be gone most of the day, but Gram is still here for you if you need anything.*

I half expected her not to show, but her magic surged through mine, as powerful and balanced as ever.

Good thing, too. The sudden press of concern and anxiety from the family made my stomach upset. I kept my own power calm, steady, level and they soon relaxed though their clinginess gave me the willies.

Safe travels, coven leader. Gram's mental voice gave away none of her own worries.

I let them go, softening the connection before I cut it off. Not completely. Never completely. I was their leader and they were with me always. But enough I could have my own thoughts, my own life. Back to the usual.

Gram's mind caressed me before she cut me off abruptly.

Sign firmly in place again. Gotcha.

Dad stepped into the middle of the pentagram, close to his effigy. I moved to join him, Meira and Sassafras already crossing the space when hands grabbed me and held me back. I turned to see Charlotte's face compressed into a tense mask of stress, her blue eyes pleading with me.

For the first time I felt it, the thin and shallow thread of magic holding her to me. But not me to her. This attachment thing she'd created when she swore herself to me was a one way street. No wonder I hadn't been aware. But it was crystal clear to me now as she stood there, shaking, the wolf inside her flashing in her eyes over and over as she fought for control of herself.

"You can't go." Roughness colored her words, a half growl echoing softly from her chest. "You can't."

I glanced at Mom who nodded, face grim, and slowly approached my bodywere.

"I have to, Charlotte." I hugged her on impulse, was surprised she didn't stiffen and pull away, but sank against me. "It's going to be okay. I'll be back soon."

"No," Charlotte said, voice firm, hands tightening as she pulled away and latched onto me. "I won't allow it."

Mom was closer, focused on the girl, moving slowly, clearly not wanting to startle her.

"We could cut the connection," I said. "Then you would be free."

Charlotte's whole body jerked so violently I cried out from her grip on me.

"Never," she snarled.

Oh dear.

What would my leaving do to her? I had no idea what the magic she'd created meant, not really. Why had I never explored it before? Suddenly worried, I met Mom's eyes. She settled her hands on Charlotte's shoulders, letting her power envelope the werewolf girl.

Charlotte sighed softly and stepped back. The connection was still there if I really hunted for it, but Mom had somehow dulled the edges, calming Charlotte down.

"You'd better go now," Mom said. "I'll take care of her."

"Will it hurt her?" I hesitated one last moment. The last thing I wanted was to damage the weregirl.

Mom frowned a little, focusing before shaking her head. "I don't believe so," Mom said. "Just make her unhappy for a while."

Charlotte's eyes flickered to wolf again and she seemed to struggle a little in Mom's grip.

Right. Time to go.

"Okay," I said, "but when I get home tonight, we're looking into this. I've put it off for too long."

Mom nodded and drew Charlotte closer even as I turned and joined Dad and my sister, demon cat poised at my feet.

"Be well," Mom said, sadness in her voice, but a little smile on her face, a real smile. "Take care of them, Harry."

"I will, my love." One of Dad's big hands settled on my shoulder, the other holding Meira to him. "We'll be back soon."

I felt him reach for the veil, added my power to his. This was no simple parting to slide inside and ride it where I wanted to go on my plane. Cutting through to Demonicon took a great deal of power. Dad's movements back and forth were easier because it was only his spirit traveling. To get Meira and I across in our physical bodies would take much more.

I was surprised then to find how easily the veil parted for us, until I felt an answering magic on the other side. Had to be Theridialis, Sassy's father, giving us the energy boost we needed to break through.

Just as we slid toward it, I felt Quaid's mind reach for mine, but it was too late, far too late to find out what he wanted. Besides, as the veil sealed around me, I was pretty sure I wouldn't have been able to hear him over the sound of Charlotte howling.

I'd crossed enough times I was used to the falling feeling in the pit of my stomach, the way everything wobbled slightly as my feet found solid ground again. At least I didn't have to pitch forward onto my hands and knees and puke this time.

That would have sucked. Not because I cared if Theridialis saw me throw up. He'd been my main witness the first time it happened. But because his tower laboratory wasn't as empty as the previous times I'd visited.

Meira wobbled next to me, but Dad's firm grip on her saved her from a face-plant. Damn, hadn't I warned her? Maybe. I guess there was no real way to adequately explain the experience. One had to go through it personally. I was pretty impressed she was upright and a little jealous, to be honest.

All of those thoughts flickered and fluttered through my mind as I tried to grasp the large group of what looked like guardsmen and the tall, slender female demon standing next to Theridialis. Sassy's father looked rather uncomfortable even as the woman surged forward with a huge smile, her black hair tied severely at the nape of her neck, tiny triangles of gemstones winking from her right cheek. She wore a flowing gown of gold and red floating from her like a cloud, though the tall and imposing collar seemed slightly ridiculous.

"My Prince." She bowed deeply. "You're arrived at last." She clapped her hands before her, long, thick, black nails clattering together as she observed us with her amber eyes. "Delightful. You must be Sydlynn." She grasped for my hand, squeezed it. My eyes traveled to our physical connection, noting I once again assumed my demon persona. I glanced at my sister, for a moment wondering if maybe life's irony had taken control. Since she looked like a demon at home, having to hide her reddish skin and cute little black horns, did that mean she would actually appear as a human here?

Lucky for her, she was as adorably demonish as ever. Though for some reason she seemed even more mature. What would being on Demonicon do to us both?

Only one way to find out.

Dad stepped in front of us as the woman tried to reach for Meira. "What is the meaning of this?" He waved at the collection of guards in their matching Roman-like outfits.

They even wore swords across their backs, though each was easily a full head taller than me and broader in the shoulder than Dad. Did they breed them to look alike?

Wouldn't have doubted it.

"Ruler requested an escort to the banquet for you and her grandchildren." The demon woman hesitated, face crumpling as though torn between orders. Theridialis grunted softly and shook his head ever so slightly at Dad.

But he wasn't taking the warning, if indeed it was one, even as my butterflies had babies and multiplied. "Banquet?" Dad's chest swelled as he echoed my own mental question in that one word, the demon in him much more lively here on Demonicon. "This was to be a private lunch with Ruler."

The woman beamed. "Oh, it is!" She smiled at us, genuinely happy to have an answer she was sure would soothe him, at least from her expression. "Only the family."

Dad groaned, shook his head. "The family," he said, voice strained.

That had to be bad.

"And a very few close friends." She pushed past him, observed us a moment. "Forgive my rudeness, I am Pagomaris, first aide to Ruler. I'm thrilled to have you both here. It's my responsibility to ensure you are presentable for the parade."

Presentable? Parade?

Dad gurgled something, face even redder than normal, but Theridialis put his hand on his arm and started whispering to him in a low voice as the demon woman went on.

"Everyone is so excited to meet you." She turned and clapped, a pair of young female demons dressed more simply than her scurrying forward with armloads of what appeared to be cosmetics, jewelry and the most elaborate clothing I'd ever seen. "Shall we begin?"

I'm not normally a stubborn person. Okay, stop laughing. But something about the woman's attitude ramped me up to dig in my heels so hard I expected the stone floor to split under me.

"No," I said.

Pagomaris turned back, the two girls joined by two others. And two others. How many helpers did we need? "I'm sorry, my dear? What did you say?"

Meira's hand slid into mine as I scowled and repeated myself. "No."

Dad's grin flashed so fast I almost missed it as he hid his mouth behind one hand.

Pagomaris hesitated, smile fading a little, same worry returning to her eyes. "We must prepare you for the parade," she repeated as if she'd been programmed. "Ruler awaits you at the Seat."

"That's nice for Ruler," I said, adopting Gram's favorite tone of voice and seeing Dad twitch with amusement. "But we're here for a private lunch with our grandmother, not to be decorated and shown off like possessions."

Pagomaris faltered, glancing at Dad and Theridialis. "But, we must." She turned back to me, trying another smile, clearly not prepared for defiance. "Ruler ordered it."

"Well, that's a shame," I said. "But she can't have everything she wants, can she?"

Even the guards gasped. Pagomaris looked like I slapped her.

"She is Ruler." Like that meant everything.

"She's my grandmother," I said. "And if she wants to see me, she can ask nicely."

The poor demon aide stuttered even as the guards shifted and looked dangerous. If they were thinking about making me, they could just take a flying leap.

"Fine," I said, turning away, looking at Dad. "Let's go home."

"Oh, no, please, you can't!" Pagomaris lunged for me, took my free hand. "Ruler will be most displeased." Was that real fear now? What kind of monster was my grandmother?

"Oh, yes we can." Dad gestured for me to join him. "Any time you're ready, sweethearts."

Syd. I stopped in preparation to move as Sassy's mind touched mine. I'd almost forgotten about him, spotting him at last standing beside his father, silver fur vibrating as his amber eyes flashed. *You can't leave.*

Why not? Dad was prepped and ready, but Theridialis looked concerned. From someone whose default expression was jovial good humor, it was a wakeup call. *Consequences?*

Not to you, Sass sent. *But for Harry.*

He doesn't seem to care. Dad's amber eyes locked on mine, as determined to take me home as I was to go.

Of course he doesn't, Sass sent. *He loves you both and wants to protect you. But your grandmother will make things very uncomfortable for him if you refuse. Ahbi Sanghamitra is not the most forgiving demon.*

Read between the lines, big trouble for Dad. And he'd had enough of that in his life in the past few years.

I squared my shoulders and faced Pagomaris. "I choose what I wear," I said. "And don't for a second think I'm waving and smiling."

Her thrilled expression told me I was totally screwed.

The dress was... ugly. All kinds of butt ugly, in my honest opinion. Like anyone else cared about what I thought. Especially Pagomaris who instead just went into demonic raptures over both Meira and I. Dressed like twins. In what felt and looked like patent leather cut out in really uncomfortable places with some kind of steel mesh. Like, awkward and embarrassing places. I kept jerking down on the bodice in an effort to hide a little more of my chest. It seemed demon fashion was more about what you showed than what you didn't.

At least all the really important bits were covered. Especially in Meira's case. No way was I letting the over-enthusiastic aide turn my little sister into some kind of child porn star.

Hopefully I wasn't the only one. But from Dad's scowl and constant pacing, he was just pissed off in general. Fair enough.

The platform boots felt like the softest silk on the inside

and I had to admit were very comfortable. Tottering around six inches above the ground? Not so much. The thick bands wrapped around my wrists made the bones ache, the black fabric, if it was fabric, so shiny I saw my disgusted face in it.

One of the helpful dressing girls draped a cape over my shoulders, fastened with a huge black flower I didn't recognize, her partner dangling what looked like a lantern from around my neck. Jewelry on Demonicon sucked.

When they tried to liberate my pentagram necklace, I drew a very firm line. With a buffet of power so harsh it sent both girls stumbling back three paces.

"Keeping it," I snarled.

"Yes, lady," they chirped.

My hair piled up around a metal cone until it was almost as tall as I was. Yes, I'm exaggerating. Still. But when they tried to slather on a coating of shellac so thick I felt like passing out from the lack of oxygen, I simply stepped away and crossed my arms over my chest, flushing a little as I realized doing so flashed more skin than I was willing to uncover.

The mirror I was placed in front of showed me a very unhappy demon girl with horns longer than Meira's, face very red despite the makeup, though I wondered if it was the makeup or just my irritation. Glittery amber eyes, narrowed in frustration. My long, thick, black nails tapped against the skirt of my hideous ensemble, shoulders wider than human, chest definitely fuller. Not that I was flat chested or anything, but my demon had some ta-tas to rival an underwear model. And muscles, more defined than home, like some kind of magical transformation as I crossed over turned me into a female wrestler.

At least under all the demonness I still kind of looked like myself, cheekbones, jaw line, long hair. But aside from one short time my demon had been outside me, this was the first real look I had at my alternate form with inhabiting it.

If it wasn't for the butt-ugly outfit, I was actually attractive in a scary chick, kick ass kind of way. Not that admitting it made me any happier with the situation.

"Can we just get this ridiculous charade over with, please?" I glared at Dad like this was his fault, even though I knew it wasn't. My gaze shifted to Sass. Right. Wrong target. But balefully staring at my demon cat got me nothing.

"Of course!" Pagomaris clapped her hands, the girls scurrying off as Meira came to stand next to me. The aide leaned in and smiled, her amber eyes very wide, teeth bared in a huge smile. "But I think you meant parade." She tweaked my cheek and turned, sweeping her way out of the room and leaving her servants to clean up the mess of dressing screens and clothing piles she'd littered Theridialis's lab with in the search for the perfect outfits.

Dad stepped forward, offering his arm and I took it, mostly because I needed him to make sure I didn't fall over.

"This is nuts," I hissed.

"I know," he said. "I should have known she'd pull something like this."

He was so grim I started to feel bad. After all, what was the big deal anyway? My grandmother was Ruler after all and a little parade and dress up? Small price to pay if it meant things went well for Dad.

"Who knows," I said, trying a smile, "it might be fun?"

Meira grinned at me from Dad's other side and had to be thinking the same thing. Come to think of it, she hadn't protested even a little bit. Maybe my sister was more suited to this place than I was. But the least I could do for Dad was put on a bit of a show if that was what it took to make my grandmother happy.

I'd only been outside once, on the large balcony down the hall from Theridialis's lab. And from very far above the city. What I remembered of it had stunned me with its beauty and as we stepped onto a wide platform on yet another balcony, I admired the view with a twinge of something unfamiliar making me uncomfortable. Vertigo, what the hell? Since when? I didn't have time to consider where my fear of heights had suddenly come from, not while I let out a little shriek and clutched at Dad as the platform suddenly fell out from under us.

Sassy's laughter made me furious. He perched at my feet, not looking at me. "Elevator," he said with a nasty little chuckle.

He was lucky I was so wobbly or he'd be finding out how far one of my boots could send him flying.

The platform stopped softly, but abruptly. Stomach in my throat, happy to be on the ground, I let Dad take the lead, guiding me forward, Meira and Sass on either side, toward the large group of guards and the eagerly waving Pagomaris. She stood on what looked like a floating disc, with dangling materials matching what I wore hanging from the edges. It bounced slightly as she gestured for us to join her as the guards fanned out on foot in front, beside and behind what had to be our vehicle.

I gingerly stepped up, feeling the platform give slightly under my weight. But the moment both feet settled on its surface the sensation of bobbing faded.

"Cool." I hopped back half a step as Pagomaris fanned her hands outward and four blobs rose from the flat base, forming into throne-like chairs, three in a line, one behind.

A fifth smaller seat, more a bed than a chair, extended from the biggest one. For Sassy, I assumed.

He proved me right by hopping immediately into his place of honor and flipping his tail around his paws, whiskers twitching. Was he annoyed or happy? It was hard to tell with him sometimes.

Pagomaris latched onto me and seated me on one side of the central throne while Meira slid into the right. Dad took the center, his only nod to the aide's need for us to dress up a thick black robe draped over his simple dark brown pants and tunic. Sass was on my side, at least, so I could pick his brain as we went.

The street had been blocked off, it seemed, more guards holding back a crowd up ahead as I finally paid attention to where we were going. The street below me was a pale pink rock, the same color as most of the city, though the glass and color of the windows and roofs made for a startlingly colorful contrast. The shadow of a large mountain, sheered almost completely off so it climbed from the ground to the sky in one continuous unbroken vertical line, loomed ahead.

"It's all magic, of course," Sassy said, voice soft as Pagomaris took the small seat in the back of the platform and clapped her hands. We moved forward, though I found my instinctual clenching to keep from being jerked ahead as we did so was unnecessary.

"You're inside a field," he said. "Same as the elevator. Pay attention."

I'd heard that particular admonishment from my grandmother enough times I felt my annoyance rise he'd adopted it too, but I let it go.

Not much choice, considering. I was suddenly overwhelmed by the rush of sound coming toward me. Or we were approaching it. Whatever the case, as the platform began to move, the crowd started to roar.

"I hope they are happy to see us." I shifted in the comfortable chair forming to me every time I moved, acutely aware of the endless eyes staring at me, the open mouths screaming, the waving arms as the crowd of watching demons went crazy.

Holy.

"Indeed they are." Pagomaris leaned forward, wiggled her fingers. The sound suddenly dimmed as though she'd adjusted the volume on a television. "All of Demonicon is thrilled you have finally come home."

Dad growled something, but I missed it as Pagomaris sat back and returned the sound to normal.

We hovered about three feet off the ground, easily

seeing over the heads of most of the demons, our guard in precise marching order around us as we wound our way through the city. Though I was a bit overcome with their enthusiasm, it wasn't long before I broke free of the influence of so much energy aimed at me and noticed we weren't any closer to the mountain, but were instead moving away from it.

"I thought the Seat was up there?" I glanced at Dad whose scowl did nothing to dampen the watcher's excitement.

"It is," Sass said. "Ahbi Sanghamitra clearly wants to show you off to all twenty-nine planes."

"We're going to other planes?" I looked around, startled. There'd been no mention of traveling across the veil. But Sass just snorted.

"Not like that," he said. "It's been a long time since the planes were separate."

I stared at him like he'd lost his mind. "What?"

Sass sighed, clearly frustrated. "Think of the planes as different areas of a city." He swished his tail at me. "The planes now only refer to where you live in Ostrogotho, the capital, and the four other major cities here on Demonicon. Because we're the capital, the highest planes are here."

Dad finally joined the conversation as I caught myself smiling a little and waving. Just couldn't help myself. The gathered demons we floated past looked so happy and excited to see us their energy was contagious. Meira was having less trouble adjusting, imperiously waving back while she giggled behind her free hand.

"There was a time," Dad said, deep voice penetrating the roar of the crowd, "when the planes were separate. Ancient demon scientists combined them using powerful magic to unify us into one larger plane."

"Milanseme is to the west." Pagomaris poked her head between the thrones. Of course she'd been listening in. I had to get used to the fact it was likely we wouldn't have much time alone here. "Our second most prestigious city."

"Thirty to seventy-five," Sassy said, keeping up his side commentary as Pagomaris listed the cities of Demonicon.

"Bilhaeder is next, to the north, stunning in summer."

"Seventy-six to two hundred."

"Ilogabon is to the east, a lovely place."

"Two hundred and one to four hundred."

"What about the other planes?" I was half joking. How many were there?

Pagomaris made a tsking sound. "They live in the countryside," she said like they had no value.

"Four-oh-one to infinity," Sassy said.

I wondered what it would take to be a demon of a plane

so lowly ranked. Then again, I was fairly certain the knowledge would make me furious.

The platform turned, winding up another street, this time a straight shot over a wide and majestic looking thoroughfare big enough to march an army through.

"The Parade," Pagomaris said with reverence in her voice. "We're almost home, girls."

Dad grunted, hands fisted in his lap.

"We could just hop into the veil and get this over with." I winked at Dad who met my eyes and shook his head.

"Against the law," he said. "Damn, I should have warned you, Syd." He ran one hand over his face, suddenly tired. "I didn't expect you to have to deal with any of this."

"No foreign magic either," Sassy said, ears flickering around as though searching for danger. But what danger could there be? We were surrounded by guards.

"Good to know." I settled back in my seat, no longer impressed with the waving crowds, those now watching of higher status, clearly. More observing us as though we were fish in a bowl, whispering to each other, though still offering smiles and waves of their own. I wanted to get this over with and go the hell home. I was already tired of the show.

But it wasn't over yet.

The platform came to a halt at the base of the mountain, the side smooth as glass. I disembarked with the help of a guard who released me into a tunnel of more of his kind, like a demon funnel to my destination. At least I didn't have to stand around wondering what to do next, though the heavy-handed controls were beginning to grate.

The guards formed a semi-circle around the next platform, another elevator by my guess, while we mounted the bouncing disc and waited for Pagomaris to do her thing.

I nearly jumped out of my skin when a fanfare of what sounded like horns went off all around me as we rose majestically from the ground, the crowd below now waving and calling out with much more enthusiasm. I swallowed hard several times as the distance increased, having a hard time looking down. The view was brilliant, spectacular, but I had to turn sideways at last and look at Dad's chest so I didn't have to admit I was terrified.

Cat claws caught my leg and I bent automatically to scoop Sassy up.

"You can't fall," he whispered. "The whole platform is shielded. You could fling yourself at the edge and— "

"Thanks for the visual," I said.

"I didn't know you were afraid of heights." His amber eyes sparkled. Great, something for him to use against me.

"I didn't think I was." True, I had trouble in the past, minor trouble, but I'd never been in a situation like this one before.

As long as I didn't puke on my polished platform boots, I'd survive.

I looked up, hoping that would help calm my nerves, to see the top rapidly approaching. I turned to face the wall, grateful for the excuse to no longer look out over the massive city, now a latticework of structured streets and moving bits of things that could have been people.

Gulp.

The platform came to a halt, smooth again, but just as swift and I stepped off with great relief onto the solid ground of the top of the mountain. It was as slick and polished as its side, as though someone had taken the peak off completely. I looked up over what had to be some kind of throne room, open to the sky. Though now I could feel the hum of wards and knew the entire place was shielded. Still freaky, but I was far enough from the edges I kept my stomach under control.

It had to be the length of a football field to the center of the peak and the two huge thrones carved of mottled black rock. Pagomaris snapped her fingers and a line of guards formed to funnel us yet again down the polished stone way.

Not like we needed the direction. It was pretty clear where we were heading. I glanced around, but did my best to keep my face straight ahead, especially after Sassy hissed at me.

"Whatever you do," he whispered, "never show fear."

Wasn't this my family? Why would they care if I was afraid? Until I got a good look.

Dad's family wasn't the handful of smiling aunts, uncles and cousins I'd been expecting. Not even close. Instead, we were greeted by a horde dressed in as elaborate fashion as Meira and I. There had to be hundreds of them, lining both sides of the walk just past where the guards stopped, crowding the aisle to the thrones in their multicolored garb, talking behind their hands as they watched.

No waving here, no smiles. Just an army of amber eyes staring us down. Even Meira's back stiffened, face composed. I hoped Sassy managed to warn her, too.

It was pretty clear as we drew near the thrones we weren't in happy company. The press of curiosity wasn't nearly as strong as their animosity.

If they didn't want us here, why were we?

The explanation sat on the tallest throne, her amber eyes watching, flat and cold, staring right through me as my grandmother watched me approach.

Pagomaris strode forward, in the lead for the first time since we stepped off the platform below, and genuflected so deeply to the thrones before her I'm positive her nose touched the stone. She then turned and smiled at me, body vibrating with joy.

"Bow now before our High and Noble Rulers," she said in a voice throbbing with emotion. "His Royal Highness, Prince Vandelarius, Ruler of the Second Seat, Demon Lord of Milanseme, Carrier of the Sacred Shroud, Lord Master General of the Guard…"

She went on so long I felt my brain going numb.

I know, Sassy sent. *Tiresome, aren't they? Your grandmother's titles could fill a thousand paged book, so get that glaze out of your eyes and listen up.*

Smartass cat.

Pagomaris finally wound down, adding one last title about a Glorious Chalice of something or another before she turned and bowed herself to the demon on the smaller throne.

It sat just below my grandmother's, to the left side, not quite as grand. In it slumped a portly demon who appeared to be in his late twenties, though I was well aware demon ages were very deceptive. More likely he was a couple of thousand years old.

1894, I think, Sassy sent.

Nitpicker.

My point was, despite all the fancy-schmancy titles he carried around with him, Vandelarius seemed frumpy and more than a little petulant, his elaborate robe crumpled in his lap, dirty boot bobbing over his crossed knee. His amber eyes sunk into his face, peering pig-like over his rounded cheeks, thick lips almost grossly so. His black hair had thinned, leaving him a severe widow's peak, scalp shining through the carefully combed remains.

By the way, Sassy sent. *You should probably bow right about now.*

What? I glanced around, so focused on my observations I missed the fact everyone else was on their knee. Dad glanced up at me, a little grin pulling his lips, but I figured I'd better conform just in case.

It sucked and I hated bowing right away. But I did it, if only for Dad.

I rose with the rest of the demons as Pagomaris turned with another huge smile.

He's Harry's brother-in-law, Sassy said while the aide beamed all around. *Married to his sister.*

My uncle. Okay then.

Watch him. Sassy's voice hissed in my mind as Pagomaris began to introduce my grandmother.

Got to love family.

"And now, all hail our Most Noble and Righteous Ruler, First Seat Ahbi Sanghamitra, Glorious Leader of all Demonicon, Salvation of…"

Um, yeah. Booooring.

A yawn began in the back of my throat and crawled its way up to my mouth as Pagomaris went on and on and bloody on until I found myself clamping my lips together to keep the damned thing in, eyes watering as the yawn crested and finally left me.

If this was what life here was like, I was happy to go home.

My eyes kept wandering, over the assembled watchers, my demon family, to Vandelarius and his clear disregard for the ceremony of it all as he scratched absently under his robe and didn't bother to hide his own yawn, mouth gaping every two minutes or so, showing the black depths of his throat and the golden molars way in the back.

Made it hard to hold back my own yawns with him shoving it in my face. As for my grandmother, I didn't really think staring at her would be the best course of action considering how everyone treated her, so I only caught glimpses as my gaze flickered to her over and over again, forming a final picture while Pagomaris finally wound down.

One thing, my grandmother was a very large woman. Not in fat, in stature. She had to stand at least as tall as Dad, if not taller, her wide shoulders a challenge to his own. Her stern face was rock-like, faintly lined, the first older demon I'd ever seen. Carefully coiffed steel-silver hair wound around her head and cascaded in perfect coils over her shoulders, falling over her massively spectacular robe and trailing down the seat to swing softly near her feet. Her eyes were the same penetrating amber of all demons, but I sensed a hardness to her making me think she was way more effigy than demon.

She didn't twitch, barely seemed to breathe the entire time, large hands clamped onto the arm rests of her throne, beak-like nose curved downward over lips thinned to a straight line. If it weren't for my previous experience, for the danger I'd endured and survived, I might have been afraid of her.

Okay. Was a little. But it wasn't like she planned to bite me. Not that anyone mentioned.

Come to think of it, how much did I know about demon culture? Was biting involved?

Syd. Get a grip.

At least the stares and whispers served me well. The more the gathered family judged me, the angrier I grew. My demon was happy to hum her dissatisfaction with present circumstances, though she was as fearful of my grandmother as I was. Shaylee stayed out of it, though I wasn't sure if on purpose or not. She felt muffled inside me, as though being on the demon plane held her back. I hadn't noticed last time, but then I was focused on saving Dad so it was likely I wouldn't have.

As for the vampire essence, she lay coiled in my heart, as usual, observing. She hadn't so much as whispered to me in the last few months, content to exist within me. Even visits from Uncle Frank and Sunny didn't rouse her much, though they still suffered from a bit of attraction to me because of her presence. I hadn't seen Sebastian and worried he was avoiding me for the same reason.

So my demon and I it was. Good enough. We could handle things, especially now I knew I wasn't allowed to use my other magicks anyway.

I snapped back to reality from my wandering thoughts to find my eyes locked on my grandmother's. She stared back, cold and empty, but this time I wasn't scared. She reminded me of Charlotte when the weregirl was in guard mode.

Good then. Pull your attempt at being creepy and hard assed, Nanny-mine. I could take it.

Pagomaris bowed again to the thrones before backing away, still nearly prone, a creepy display reminding me of a giant metal spider. She didn't rise until she was almost to us. Before she could speak again, Sassafras darted forward, leaping up the three stairs to my grandmother's throne and hopping up into her lap.

A smile. Was it? Could that concrete face really smile? One huge hand lifted from its place on the throne, almost as if a statue come to life, and she stroked his fur with amusement pulling her lips upward.

"Sassafras," she said, voice deep, but very feminine. "How delightful to see you, dear boy."

He began to purr, the sound of it carrying even as his demon magic reached me, woven into his own personal song. "Ahbi," he said.

Gasps of shock. Clearly her first name wasn't the best choice of address. Even Pagomaris blanched, paling under her red-tinted skin.

But my grandmother laughed, a booming echo, still gently stroking his fur.

"Welcome home, boy," she said as her eyes lifted to me.

So she had a heart. Somewhere inside her, anyway. And now, thanks to Sass, I knew it.

You're welcome, he sent in a very tight thread. *But don't get cocky. She'll crush you like a bug.*

I was sure he was full of it, but why risk it?

Because she gave me reason to.

"Approach, Meira, daughter of Haralthazar, Demon Prince of the Second Plane." My grandmother didn't gesture, face falling again into a cold mask.

My sister moved ahead without a sound or hesitation while my blood began a slow burn.

Um, she was much more than Dad's daughter. Much more. The group surrounding us laughed behind their hands, as if aware of the slight. Coldness I could handle. Arrogance when it came to my lineage?

She had another freaking thing coming.

Any fear I'd felt, any residual concern, melted like cheap wax under the rumble of my rising temper. Even my demon joined me, snapping fire through my body until I was rigid with it.

Two could play this game, oh yeah. As Meira bowed to our grandmother and accepted whatever platitude the old demon offered, I ran over my plan in my head until it was perfect.

I quivered inside, but stood a statue myself on the outside when Meira finally backed away and my grandmother fixed me once again with a gaze like steel.

Let's see how she liked a taste of her own medicine.

They wanted scandal? Something to gasp at? I was more than happy to deliver.

Before she could say a word, I stepped forward and opened my big mouth.

"Considering you seem to be misinformed," I said, "allow me to clear up the issue and introduce myself." My demon growled behind my words as every single pair of eyes latched onto me and refused to let go. The pressure was unbelievable, but my temper carried me onward, for good or ill. "I am Sydlynn Thaddea Hayle, leader of the Hayle coven, daughter of Miriam Hayle, Leader of the North American Witches Council. I am also Sydlynn, demon child of Haralthazar, Prince of the Second Plane." I paused a moment, ignoring the open-mouthed shock of the family, the way Pagomaris's hands fluttered ineffectually as though her worst nightmare had come to life, only focused on the steady, steely gaze of my grandmother. "I am Shaylee, Princess of the Sidhe Seelie Court. And I am the essence of all vampires, born of the maji." As I ran through the list of my personas, I felt a shiver of pride. Not because I was powerful—I was, without question—but for the first time in my life

I recognized and acknowledged publicly the honor of who I actually was, the lives I carried inside me, and it all finally hit me.

Whoa. How cool was I?

Grandmother didn't seem all that impressed and from the sudden rumble of anger and shock rippling through the family, I hadn't made any friends with my little proclamation. But I refused to back down, buoyed by the grim smile on Dad's face and the fact Sassafras hadn't mentally chastised me yet.

Let them think what they wanted. I was Sydlynn Hayle and damned proud of it.

Grandmother let the chatter go on for a moment before raising her right hand. The sudden silence felt like she'd numbed my ears. Not once did she blink or turn her gaze from me, amber fire eating away at the edges of my resolve despite my best intentions. Now that my temper had cooled somewhat, I realized the position I'd put myself in. Front, center. Yay me. Brilliant move, Syd. And yet, my sense of pride didn't leave me and so I remained where I was, back straight, head up and heart beginning to beat a little faster the longer she stared me down.

Before I could cave under the weight of her gaze, Grandmother gestured, again with her right hand, motioning me forward. Another gasp, this time without anger, only pure surprise and I knew I'd won.

This round. Good thing I was going home soon.

"Welcome, granddaughter." She purposely left out every single name I'd used, but I didn't argue. What was her game now? "Your family has long despaired at your absence and that of your sister."

Yeah, sure they had. I could just feel the sickly sweet love and compassion oozing from my relatives. Any more attention from them and I'd likely end up with a terminal case of adoration overload.

Grandmother went on as if she spoke utter truth. "It is wonderful to have you both home with us at long last and we hope you enjoy all being children of the ruling family has to offer."

Careful, Sassy sent very softly, that tight band of connection so weak it barely reached me. He was being uber cautious, clearly. *We're getting to the real reason you're here. Don't piss her off further until we know what she wants.*

Then I can finish the job? No idea why I was feeling so cocky.

We'll see. Sassy's chuckle was full of venom. *That was absolutely brilliant, by the way. Don't ever do anything like that again.*

We'd see.

Grandmother gestured for Meira to join me and I felt my sister slide in beside me. I half expected her little hand to slide into mine, but it never happened. Of course. That would be a show of weakness and Meira, as young as she was, clearly understood the stakes here, even if I was only beginning to.

What kind of family did Dad have? I wasn't really liking them much and I didn't even know them.

"Now is the time for your plane selection," Grandmother said. Sassy's mind jabbed me so violently I almost jumped, though there were no words, only a spike of fear I was sure he never intended to reach me.

"I protest, Ruler." Dad stepped forward immediately, to stand at my sister's side. "Neither of my daughters are born of this plane. And considering they will be departing in a few short hours, plane assignments are unnecessary."

Grandmother glared at him. "You would deny your own daughters their status, Haralthazar?" She tapped the fingers of her left hand on the arm of her throne even as Vandelarius glared at Dad with pure venom. "It is the decree of the Seat no demon child shall be without status."

"So decreed," Vandelarius said. Hissed, more like. His

voice was kind of whiny, not that I was surprised, high pitched. Made my skin do a creepy crawly dance.

Dad hesitated, looked like he wanted to argue. Finally fell back with a grunt, face frozen in anger.

This is really important, Sassy sent. *Pay close attention. Ahbi's real goal is right here, in the plane assignments.*

Whatever that meant.

Grandmother turned her gaze to my sister. "Meira," she said in a ringing voice, power reaching forward from her to envelop my sister, "I rename you Hathenemeira, and declare you a Lady of the Seventh Plane."

Meira gasped softly as the power snapped into place, her eyes flaring with light before she bowed her head to our grandmother.

Muttering. Dark looks. My heart, now beating faster than normal, did an odd jump making my chest hurt. What was the big deal? Dad used to be a seventh plane demon. Kind of made sense Meira would be too. The renaming thing kind of annoyed me, but why were most members of the family now staring at my sister like she was the enemy?

Syd, Sassy sent. *This is very bad. Very, very bad.*

If Sassafras was nervous, I had good reason. As Grandmother turned to me, I felt her power wrap around me, chill for demon fire, normally full of heat. Curious and on impulse I traced her magic back to her, hoping for some insight, only to meet with a massive wall of amber stone, shields built and reinforced for literally centuries.

But her power wasn't alone. I traced a second source to her left, found Vandelarius's magic hiding behind hers, probing me, checking me out. I jabbed back with some anger, felt him retreat. He might have been second seat, but he wasn't nearly the demon she was and it would seem he wasn't prepared to openly challenge me or my sister at this point.

Ah, family love. Wonderful, wasn't it?

Grandmother's power tightened around me like a blanket, bringing goose bumps to the surface of my flesh. "Sydlynn," Grandmother said, "I rename you Sydlynhamitra."

More gasps, wide eyes, shaking of heads. I was sure Sass or Dad would explain why when this charade was over even as Grandmother's power leeched inside me. My demon struggled suddenly, bound, though the amber fire could do nothing against Shaylee and the vampire, nor the other four elements I controlled. I felt them push Grandmother back. She retreated to only my demon who finally relented, though in that moment I was well aware if Ahbi Sanghamitra wanted to push me, it was likely I'd be a crushed smear on the floor.

Grandmother's lips curled into a partial smile, her massive presence hovering over me.

"Well met, Sydlynhamitra," she said. "For your strength and the purity of your power, I declare you a Princess of the Second Plane."

10

I knew I was in trouble the moment the words left her mouth. The stunned silence meeting most of the afternoon's revelations so far was shattered by a chorus of protests, both from my father's now agitated and angry family, and from Dad and Sassafras.

My demon cat leaped free of Grandmother's lap only to spin and glare at her. "Preposterous," he said. "You can't assign her so high a position."

Grandmother's eyes tightened just a little bit, but her voice carried the weight of her power. "I can," she said, voice a rumble of thunder, "and I have."

That quieted the masses, but Sassy simply sank to the ground with his ears flat back, a soft growl emerging from him. "She is untried," he said even as Dad, his face now showing just how angry he was, put himself between me and Grandmother.

"What have you done, Mother?" His body shook slightly as his anger rippled from him in waves. "What is the meaning of this?"

I slipped around him, refusing to be cut out of the conversation even as Grandmother fixed my father with her cold amber eyes. But this time it wasn't she who spoke.

"You again question Ruler." Vandelarius's voice made me want to punch something. Preferably his ugly face. "An unseemly habit, Prince Haralthazar. And a dangerous one."

Dad ignored him. "Surely you're aware what this game means for my daughters?"

Grandmother finally showed real emotion, a storm of feelings flickering over her face, including so much frustration I thought Dad might burn up right then and there. "Had you brought your daughters to me as they developed, they would have had time to grow accustomed to their station. As it is, you've left us with no choice. None, Haralthazar." One pointed talon of a fingernail jabbed at him. "This is on your shoulders." Her gaze settled on me as her mask returned. "They are what they are, experienced or not. Now it is up to them to keep what they've been given."

Um, what? I really, really didn't like the sound of that.

Dad didn't back down right away, still rigid with anger, glaring at his mother.

"Is it time, my son?" Grandmother's smile was almost welcoming. "Have you decided to finally take your proper place at my side?"

Vandelarius did *not* look happy. In fact, his face turned so red I thought he might bust a major artery. But he remained silent, though the hate-filled stare he focused on Dad worried me.

Hey, wait a second. Proper place? At her side?

Dad was supposed to be in the throne next to her?

Worry about the whole status thing, a problem or not, faded at the thought of Dad as Second Seat. What would that mean for us, for our family? And if he was meant to rule, what happened to put his brother-in-law on the throne instead?

Dad backed up a step, breathing steady, calm returning, though I knew him well enough to see it was all a show. "I bow to your wisdom and leadership, Ruler," he said in a voice dripping sugary sweetness even as his hands tightened into fists at his side. Clearly, Dad wasn't all that great at the whole politics thing.

"You are dismissed." Grandmother surged to her feet. "Until dinner."

Everyone bowed. It was just as hard the second time. I hated feeling subordinate and being forced to show it. Made me stabby.

Pagomaris hurried to us as Grandmother, Vandelarius trailing behind her with a million or so courtiers and flunkies following, strode off further across the mountain peak while our guide ushered us back toward the elevator.

The ride down was no less puke inspiring, though we only descended one level before getting off again. Pagomaris stood aside as Dad swept open the doors to a large chamber filled with comfortable looking seating, the walls the same polished stone as the rest of the mountain, one side of it open to overlook the city.

I purposely avoided the view, wondering where my acute height issues had come from all of a sudden and tried to settle into a chair covered in some kind of red mottled leather, over stuffed and very soft. Only to rise again almost immediately and begin to pace while Dad softly spoke to a handful of demons. His servants maybe? Pagomaris just hovered as though we might need her.

Not.

I really wanted her to leave, if only so I could actually speak candidly with Dad and Sassafras. No way was I saying anything in front of her that could get back to Grandmother. I'd learned in a few short minutes before the thrones of the Seat, trust wasn't much of a way of life here and I wasn't about to play myself the fool.

Yup. Growing up. Sigh.

Theridialis hurried in, round body bouncing slightly

as he brushed past Pagomaris and nodded to Dad who finished dismissing his people. He turned and noticed the aide, scowl firmly fixed.

"That will be all," he said, voice harsher than I'm sure he meant.

"But, my Prince," she said, almost babbled really, "I must ready the Lady and Princess for the banquet. Now I know their rankings, I can dress them accordingly."

It seemed like that was the most important thing to Pagomaris. Which made me wonder if she really was a threat after all. Still, wasn't risking it.

"We're fine." I stepped toward her, herding her to the door even as she spluttered and begged me with her pleading gaze. "Come back later." Was it rude to slam the heavy portal in her face?

Yeah, I'd apologize later.

I turned back to the others with a scowl of my own, doing my best to cross my arms over my chest without exposing anything in my ridiculous getup. "Please," I said, "tell me what's going on? Because as far as I can tell, being a Princess isn't such a bad thing." I picked at the sleeve of my outfit. "Aside from the ugly clothes."

Meira grinned at me and nodded, but the tension returned to her face so I knew she took this as seriously as I did.

Sassafras answered me, grunting his way up into the chair beside Meira, front paws on her leg. "This is very serious," he said. "Your grandmother just put the two of you in a great deal of danger."

What had every single person I told back home said to me? Oh yeah. Be careful. Like I had a choice in the matter. Looked like careful had its own meaning on Demonicon. "Okay," I said. "Keep going." Voice steady? Check. Heart suddenly doing back flips? Yup.

"You remember what I told you," he said as Dad and Theridialis both took seats with heavy sighs and downcast expressions, "how I was banished and why?"

"You were fighting another demon," I said. "Stripped him of his magic." It was really all I remembered, shame on me, but it had been a pretty traumatic time and my memory wasn't the best. At least Sassy was nodding so I got that much right.

"I was fighting for status." He paused, let what he'd said sink in.

Which it finally did. "Fighting?" I dropped my arms and approached, whole body suddenly wide-awake and listening with every single pore. Even the vampire inside me perked up.

Sassy nodded. "If one wants to rise in status, you must

fight for it. Take the power of other demons—but only part of it. That was my final arrogance."

He sounded so sad I reached out and scratched his cheek while my brain whirred and clicked and made connections. I met Dad's eyes with a surge of understanding.

"You weren't given a raise," I said. "You had to fight for it."

Dad sat back, looking tired. "I didn't want your mother to know," he said. "But my return to Demonicon wasn't met with enthusiasm." So much sarcasm. "In fact, the majority of the family was disappointed I wasn't dead. I understand there were bets paid, large sums that made the winners very unhappy."

Oh. My. Swearword. What the hell kind of people were they?

"I hadn't fought in years, by choice," Dad said. "But I wasn't given a choice. First I had to defend my place on the Seventh, but that wasn't good enough for Mother." It was Dad's turn to leap to his feet and pace, hands clasped behind his back. "I spent the months after my return battling one family member after another until I reached Second Plane status."

"And then, what?" I glanced at Sassafras who hummed softly in unhappiness. "They just stopped attacking you?"

Dad nodded. "Your grandmother had what she wanted. At least, the first part."

Theridialis snorted softly, hands patting his wide belly. "Ahbi Sanghamitra will never have what she wants. That is, until you ascend the Second Seat."

"I'm not so sure now." Dad's look of concern when he focused on me made me shudder. "I fear she might have a new heir in mind."

Why was he looking at me like that? "Um, what?"

Dad shook his head even as Sassafras spoke.

"There's more to this," he said. "It's bad enough she made Syd a Second Plane Princess, but to grant her name, and not as a prefix... Ahbi hasn't given Syd a chance."

"Explain." I know it came out gruff, but I wasn't in the mood for half-truths or protecting me from what was going on.

It seemed for the first time in my life I was about to get the whole story up front without having to go hunting for it myself. Wonders never ceased. "You noticed she renamed Meira with a prefix." Sassy head-butted my sister gently. "Hathenemeira is a mix of Haralthazar and Henemordonin, your father and grandfather." Meira's hand stroked his fur as he met her eyes. "Both noble names she can be proud of."

"But me?" I caught Dad's jaw grinding as he stared at the stone floor while Sassy turned to me.

"You she gave a suffix," he said, "from her own name."

"Got that part," I said.

"Not quite," he said. "By doing so she declared you her favorite. Which means it's now open season for any demon who wants to challenge you."

"Wait, challenge me?" I'd known it was coming, I really had. But hearing it out loud, knowing now I'd have to fight, I was suddenly freaked out it was real.

"If you were to stay here with such status, with the name she gave you," Theridialis's voice reached me from where he sat, shaking his head, kind face pale, "you would be forced to fight to keep it."

"And fight and fight and fight." Sassy's golden eyes locked onto me and held me still. "Until you beat them all or you were destroyed."

Holy.

"Good thing I'm going home then, huh?" I met my sister's gaze, found her grim, but resolved.

"Will I have to fight, too?" She hugged the silver Persian.

"Only if you stay," he said. "But yes. Both of you would be forced to defend what you've never earned in the first place."

Part of me was a little stung by his words. I was pretty powerful after all. Who knew if I didn't deserve my station? But that part was pretty tiny while the rest of me wanted to hop into the veil right now and head for home, dinner or no dinner.

"You said grandfather?" Anything to distract me at this point. "Will we meet him at some point?"

No one said anything for a long moment and I wondered what I'd stumbled into. Finally, Dad broke the sad silence.

"I really should just send you two home right now."

"You can't." Sassy's sigh was so loud it snorted from his pushed-in nose. "She'll make things even worse for you, Harry. But once dinner is finished, the girls can go and you will have fulfilled your obligation."

"Until the next time she pushes me." Dad resumed his pacing. "I'm so tired of taking orders from her."

Sassy and Theridialis both gasped. "You didn't mean that, my friend." The portly scientist's eyes drifted around the room. Were we being observed somehow? Likely. And I could only imagine what Dad said was pretty much treason in such a tight-ass society.

"Dad," I said. "Where do you stand in line for the Second Seat?"

"I'm second heir," he said. "His son, Cypherion, is next

in line. If something happens to Vandelarius, he takes his father's seat and I'm made heir."

"Okay then." I hesitated before asking him my next question. "And where am I?"

Dad's eyes were sad, but he didn't pull his punch. "You're right behind me," he said.

Well, well. I really had to ask, didn't I?

The door swung open while we all absorbed the gloom of the room. Pagomaris peeked in, a desperate smile on her face.

"I really have to have the Lady and the Princess," she said.

I didn't have the strength to argue.

I had Sassy in my head, linked to Meira, the entire time Pagomaris and her squad of beautifier demons ruthlessly tugged and stuffed us into a new set of clothing.

You'll both be fine, he sent. *There shouldn't be opportunity for a fight at this point, as long as you are in the banquet. Don't accept any offers to wander off and don't agitate anyone.* He sighed. *I know that's a lot to ask of you, Sydlynn, but I'd like to deliver you to your mother in one piece.*

I scowled as Meira giggled. *So you don't think anyone will step up?* That was a big relief.

Not during the banquet, he sent. *As long as you don't push it, it's kind of frowned on.*

Good to know. I felt my shoulders unknotting as Pagomaris firmly gripped my head and stogged it into some kind of fur hat. I felt immediately itchy and wished I could get away with swatting her.

For all I knew, she'd like it.

Now, my demon cat went on as if I weren't being turned

into some kind of overly feminized Sasquatch, *if you are challenged, accept right away. No hesitation, no fear. So be prepared just in case.*

And my tension was back. Lovely.

Strike first. Meira sounded more than a little bloodthirsty, though I supposed her attitude was a good thing under the circumstances.

Exactly. His thick, silver tail thrashed once. *Nice outfit, by the way.*

I glared at him. *Shut it, smartass cat.*

If Meira's fur-clad legs, arms, head and shoulders were any indication of what I was wearing, I'd had enough.

I spun with a snarl on Pagomaris, jerking the fur hat from my head and throwing it on the floor. "I want clothes," I snapped. "Not a costume. Now." Offending body coverings followed the hat, now a pile of crumped white fur on the polished stone while Meira followed suit with a wicked grin on her face.

Pagomaris gripped her cheeks in both hands, aghast. "Your Highness!"

"I mean it." I shivered a little in the barely-there underwear she'd forced me to don, though at least I'd been allowed to change behind the screen her little people seemed to carry around with them everywhere. "Normal. Or as normal as you've got."

Sassy's laughter in my head almost made me snap.

As I was saying, he went on as Pagomaris nearly wept, clapping her hands at her servants, sending them scurrying for something suitable to my taste, *your opposition won't expect you to be ready since neither of you has experience.*

I beg to differ, I shot back. *I've been in lots of fights.* That helped me feel a little better. I'd been through a hell of a lot and managed to survive. Surely I could handle a demon or two considering the firepower I had at my disposal.

I remind you, Sass sent, stern and almost harsh, *no use of other powers. Only demon. Unless you want to be put to death?*

Oh crap. *Gotcha.*

Slash attack, Sassy sent. *Take out their shields first then work from the bottom up. Most don't expect you to attack their foundation right away. They'll be going for your core, so duck and take out the feet.*

You did this a lot. Meira's eyes lit up at the sight of the new clothes coming our way. I looked them over as Pagomaris held up what looked like a one-piece red pantsuit. Yes, it had some kind of crystals stuck all over it, but at least it seemed I could move in it. I sighed and nodded to her, bringing a smile back to the aide's face.

I did, Sassy sent. *But remember, I was a champion. It's*

likely my methods have been studied and incorporated into current fighting techniques.

I wanted to chastise him for his arrogance, except I knew he was right.

Damn it.

That means you really can't help us? I winced as Pagomaris and her horde of helpers slid me into the suit. It hadn't looked skin-tight when she held it up originally. Though it covered my whole body, there was not a thing left to the imagination. Seriously?

I didn't say that, Sassy sent. *There are no rules against having power support if you can convince another demon to help, but it never happens.* Surprising? Not. *I'm closely connected to both of you, enough I should be able to guide you if things go wrong. Oh yes, this outfit is so much better.*

Maybe I did want the fur back after all. But when Pagomaris lifted a further piece of clothing from the hands of her servant, I changed my mind. The poncho-like shape was so sheer it seemed to ripple as though alive, crusted with its own wealth of jewels along the hem and neckline. It shuddered its way over my head, falling to my feet, tickling my toes. The sleeves brushed my fingertips and, for the first time, I actually smiled back at Pagomaris with genuine happiness.

"This," I said, "is perfect."

Meira was admiring her own, a pale shade of cream. She looked amazing in it, the shimmering covering almost making her body seem blurred.

As our feet were slid into boots with four-inch platforms, hair and faces adorned with more jewels, I remembered Darin Mavore, the arrogant witch whose shields I'd shredded back at the first of term when he'd used his magic to grope me.

I've done that shield attack before, I sent to Sassy, sharing the experience with my sister.

Yes, he sent back. *Exactly. Just remember you're not dealing with some stupid young witch. The demons who challenge you are powerful and experienced.*

Meira's lips formed a grim line and I reached out in sudden concern to take her hand while activity went on around us.

It'll be okay, Meems, I sent.

I know, she sent back. *But I'm ready to fight if I have to.*

Hayle witches. Man, we were so stubborn.

I'll be right here, I sent.

Meira's eyes snapped with anger. *I can take care of myself. I'm not a baby, Syd.*

Whoa. Where did that come from?

I know, I sent. *I just… okay.*

My little sister was growing up. Damn it.

I leaned in and hugged her when her angry expression didn't fade. *I know*, I sent with love wrapped around it. *But we have to be here for each other, watch each other's backs. That's all I meant. I need you here for me, too.*

She softened immediately and hugged me so hard I could feel her heartbeat. *I love you, Syd.*

You too, Meems. We parted as Pagomaris and her brood backed off. *Are we ready?*

I turned to the aide and repeated the question out loud. The aide clapped her hands, had a mirror brought forward. It was huge, not the slim piece of glass I expected, but a triple-wide sheet two girls struggled to hold up. It threw back our reflection and, for a moment, I caught my breath.

This was us, my sister and I? These two shimmering demons, light catching on gems, throwing light at every breath? Meira looked so much older than her ten years.

And me? I looked like a princess.

Time to act like one.

12

And so the Hayle sisters rode into battle, our demon cat between us.

Dad met us in the hall outside his own quarters, on the same level as the dressing room we'd been shunted off to. Even he had changed completely this time, into what looked like a very old-fashioned version of a tuxedo—if tuxedos were made of odd fabric eddying with movement as though a living organism flowed around inside and if spikes from every joint were ever *de rigueur*.

He looked about as unhappy as we had earlier so I didn't poke fun at his porcupine outfit even as Pagomaris gushed at how wonderful he looked.

"Time to go," he growled, cutting her off.

She took the hint.

I considered taking Dad's arm again, if just for the stability of having him beside me, but at least these platform boots were flats, no real heel, and with a few careful steps I felt more confident. Besides, if I was going to literally stand on my own two feet here, if appearances were, in fact, as important as I was beginning to believe, walking into the banquet with assistance could be seen as a sign of weakness.

This was going to be a very uncomfortable meal if I had to watch every single thing I did and said. Unless I didn't do or say anything. Well, we'd see about that.

The elevator descended a further floor, depositing us into a massive open chamber just past a short, wide hallway entry. The place was massively ceilinged, more windows open to the sky, a horse-shoe shaped table dominating the center of the room. Two more tables, same shape, smaller stature, flanked it while two more, even smaller, flanked those. The smaller tables were already filled, what had to be the head table's forty or so chairs only partially taken.

Pagomaris halted at the entry, gesturing to a slim older demon in a dour black uniform closed over his throat to the tips of his fingers and toes as if he was being eaten alive by his outfit. His gray hair spiked up from his scalp as he turned to us, the amber in his eyes barely glowing. Was he so old his power had faded?

Servants have less status, Sassy sent me as though guessing my curiosity. Either that or he was eavesdropping on my thoughts. My demon chuffed in annoyance at the idea, but

I didn't call him on it. There could come a time I'd need him in my head, after all. *That means less magic. Consider that.*

Right. *So when I fight, if I lose...*

Don't lose. He cut me off as he sat, tail wrapping around his paws, looking about as if he were the most important person here.

Made me want to pick him up and snuggle him and tell him he was my favowite puddy tat ever.

The stress was clearly making me irrational.

"His Highness, Prince Haralthazar." The little old demon had pipes like a rock star. I actually started just a little as he trumpeted Dad's name into the room.

Everyone stopped talking and stared. Yippee.

"Her Highness, Princess Sydlynhamitra." The name thing had to go.

"Her most noble, Lady Hathenemeira." Meira seemed much more poised than I felt and hadn't stumbled in her stupidly high boots once.

Envy, thy name is Syd.

"And his most noble, Lord Sassafras." I almost jumped again. Wait, Sass had status? He'd been banned from Demonicon for almost killing a boy he fought. When he died, saving Dad's life, the both of them returned here and

I realized I'd never gotten the full story out of my friend. Yes, he was pardoned, I knew that much. But he was a cat. How could he have status?

There were a few whispers at the announcement, but it was obviously old news, at least to the family. I'd be digging into that particular story the moment we had time.

Later, Sassy sent.

You betcha, later.

Two young demon males in similar outfits to the door announcer leaped forward and bowed to us before turning and leading the way. I followed, head high, shoulders back, ignoring the glares and mutters while I focused on walking and not falling on my face. Stay to myself, don't do or say anything offensive and remain upright.

Just. Keep. Moving.

My new mantra. I was guided forward, my clunky shoes soundless on the stone floor, every step heavier than the last. But I made it to my seat without a problem—no tripping, no challenges.

Wicked.

The chair was massive, some kind of carved black wood with huge arm rests making me shudder to touch them. They literally looked like arms, skeletal, ending in grasping claws cupped upward. I refused to turn around and see what was carved into the top of the chair, knowing it would likely give me nightmares later and praying quietly the seat was really wood and I wasn't sitting on what remained of someone.

Ew. Just ew.

At least the table was relatively normal, made of glass over huge stone piers, though I noticed something swam in the middle when I really paid attention. Were they fish? Nasty looking creatures, multi-colored, floating in a pale liquid, swished along as though swimming in a river. I pulled free the cloth napkin placed on my plate and covered as much of the surface as I could, though I found myself grinning a little as Sassy's eyes kept glancing down at the sudden movement, tail thrashing. I gestured to him, to my spread napkin and he bowed his head with great aplomb, perching on it.

Thank you, he sent, mental voice furious. *I'd forgotten Ahbi's particular sense of humor.*

This was my Grandmother's sick idea of a joke? Yeah, not getting away with that.

I snapped my fingers and a young servant appeared instantly. "A proper seat for his lordship," I snapped.

The boy's eyes flew very wide before he bowed and vanished.

Sydlynn, Sassy sent, *while I appreciate the sentiment, you're supposed to stay under the radar.*

Screw that, I snapped back.

It's an insult, he sent, *nothing more. I think I'll live.*

He was right of course. My damned temper was going to get me in trouble again. But my demon hummed happily about me speaking up so I tried not to worry too much.

A moment later the boy reappeared with what looked like a hollowed out cushion, covered in fur. His companion cleared a setting and settled the seat in its place at my left. Sassafras stepped up and settled, nodding to the boy who bowed back.

I glanced down the table, only then missing Meira. It wasn't until I turned that I spotted her at the second tier of seats. I was suddenly so angry she'd been taken from me I almost spoke up.

Leave her, Sassy sent. *She's in her proper place.*

She's all alone. I met her eyes, felt her power on mine.

I'm okay, she sent, amber gaze sparkling. *Honest.*

Dad's hand settled on mine on my right. I glanced his way, saw the tension around his eyes while the rest of his face remained calm.

Okay then. I fixed Sassafras with a glare. *So how come you're allowed up here?*

I'm special. He groomed one paw with dedicated attention and would say nothing more.

The table filled around us after we took our seats, only two remaining empty. I tried not to fidget, grateful at least it seemed demons used the same kinds of cutlery and plates as humans so I wasn't totally lost.

"All rise." The booming voice of the announcer brought us to our feet. I stood without even thinking, the command in his tone triggering an instinctual reaction and I wondered then if he'd been magicked that way.

"His Royal Highness, Prince Vandelarius, Second Seat."

I didn't glance toward the door, but did bow with everyone else. I was going home very shortly and had to keep reminding myself of the fact. Vandelarius wandered his way down to his chair at the head of the horseshoe and plopped himself down with a bored expression.

"And her Most Royal Majesty," the announcer's voice throbbed with devotion, "Ahbi Sanghamitra, Ruler of All Demonicon."

This time I did look up. Grandmother strode toward us like a juggernaut of energy, her very presence dominating every single demon in the room. Her gaze settled on mine for a moment as she passed, me peeking through my bow, and I caught her smile at me as she did.

Hmm. Maybe my grandmother wasn't the monster I thought she was. It would have been nice to spend a moment alone with her, away from the pomp and crap. Could she be a real person under all that title?

Grandmother sat, followed by a mass scraping of chairs as everyone else took their place in response. I was a little slow and squeaked softly as the boy behind my chair shoved before I was ready. I plopped rather unceremoniously into my seat and had to suffer Sassy's glare.

"Begin," Grandmother said.

Food arrived. Boy, did it. The aromas were so amazing I found my mouth watering. I didn't recognize any of the dishes, and yet my demon seemed to know exactly what we'd like.

Piles of steaming things I could never describe followed deep bowls of some broth making my throat burn. Soft rolls of a wheat-like flour only ten times more flaky and delicious were slathered in a thick sauce tasting faintly of salt and sugar and a million other amazing spices.

I ate everything put in front of me, enjoyed every single bite. It was easy to ignore the chatter around me while I was so absorbed in the succulent food being constantly placed on my plate.

While we ate, jugglers and acrobats entertained us in the

center of the horseshoe. But they used magic to augment their performances and I knew any human of their ilk would weep in jealousy. I felt like a bumpkin country cousin finally exposed to city life, but couldn't help gaping and clapping and thoroughly enjoying myself.

Maybe this whole thing wasn't so bad after all. As dinner went on and no one spoke up to challenge or even try to prod me into doing something I shouldn't, I found my guard slipping a little, though Dad was as tense as ever.

Sassafras finally snapped in my mind. *Pay attention*, he sent. *They are lulling us into feeling safe.*

I don't know, I sent back. *Things seem pretty straight up so far, Sass. Are you sure you're not overreacting?*

The performers left, much to my disappointment. I wished I had a video camera so I could take the memory of them home with me. I was even more discouraged with their departure as the second wave of center stage entertainment started up.

Speeches. Were they serious? They followed the most amazing show I'd ever seen in my entire life with speeches? Starting with the lowest of underlings, it seemed, aiming their words at me and my sister. At Dad and Sass. Finally toward Ruler.

Oh. My. Swearword.

While the food remained delicious, I found myself going numb as demon after ranking demon rose and spoke at great length about how delighted they were we were here, how brilliant Grandmother was. Yada. Yada. Yada.

Kill me now and put me out of my misery.

It dragged on so long I finally glanced at one of the open windows and the dying light and felt a little surge of nerves. We were pushing the last of the daylight, maybe a half hour left. This really needed to wrap up so we could go home.

I'm not sure if Dad was reading my mind, but he turned to Grandmother in the middle of a speech, totally cutting off the tall female demon whose smile reminded me of a hunting shark.

"It's time," he said. "The girls must be going."

Grandmother met his eyes. "Of course." She gestured and the unhappy woman returned to her seat, clearly put out she'd been interrupted. Was she one of Dad's sisters?

Yikes.

Grandmother clapped her hands and the hall fell silent. "My granddaughters must return to their own plane." No one complained. Not surprising. "But before they go, dessert."

She rose without a word as Sassafras hissed.

This could be it, he sent while everyone else stood and

followed her toward one of the windows. I hadn't noticed the balcony before, but it was very clear to me now as I pushed myself up.

Could be what? I was about to hoist him into my arms when he hopped down on his own.

Don't touch me, he sent. *Focus. If anyone is going to challenge you, it will be during transition.*

I almost gave him a hard time for his paranoia.

Almost

"Sydlynhamitra," a burly young male demon with shoulders the size of the mountain and a body to match stepped out of the crowd heading to the balcony, his amber eyes on fire, power swirling around his hands, "I, Mobicandron, Knight of the Tenth Plane, challenge you for status."

13

I did exactly what Sassafras warned me not to do.

I hesitated.

But they sky was darkening and Meira and I had to go. This was terrible timing, the absolute worst. On purpose? Panic heated my insides and stirred my blood as I realized it was likely—not only that, I had to fight or I'd lose status. Why did I care? Not so much for me, not really. But Dad had to live here. And considering they would take part of my demon's power if I lost... in the heartbeat I had to think things through, my demon made it very clear to me losing even one smidge of her magic was unacceptable.

She took over. Probably was for the best, really, considering I couldn't get out of my own head long enough to take action. Good thing she did, too, because Mobicandron didn't wait to see if I accepted, but lashed out immediately.

My demon was fast, very fast, just fast enough as it turned out, to block the blow he'd sent my way and slash out at him in turn. For a moment, I felt a rush of confidence. I'd done this before, so no problem, right?

Only this was no Darin Mavore, no Jean Marc or Kristophe Dumont I was dealing with. The demon before me parried with precise skill and struck back almost before my demon had time to block.

Again with the almost. He was clearly practiced and had won many battles. I could feel his power, how it pulsed around him, the heat from his shields. All offense, all the time.

Defense on the other hand, wasn't getting me anywhere.

What are you doing? Sassy's voice was almost choked with fury. *Attack his sorry ass and take him down!*

He made it sound so easy. Meanwhile I was the one with my hands full.

I dodged sideways as a glowing ball of amber fire whizzed toward me, only then noticing as it impacted something surrounding us we'd been shielded from the rest of the family. Great. Trapped in a bubble of magic fighting a demon who was most likely my cousin and doing my best not to get killed.

Forget yourself, Sassy snarled. *You have to take him out! Now!*

He jabbed my demon with magic claws, making us both

cry out. But at least the shout was full of anger. It stung so much my power flared. Mobicandron chose that exact unfortunate moment to smile at me.

Oh no, he did *not*.

My temper flared as my demon magic rose in a column before me, forming a giant fist I used to battering ram him backward until he impacted the shield. He gasped for air, collapsing beneath the crushing weight I held on him, fury still beating at the inside of my head.

Now, Sassy sent. *Finish him!*

I jerked some power free, enough to create thin ribbons of magic, using them like a lash to sever his wards into strips of worthless energy. Power oozed from him to hover just above the floor as his eyes rolled back in his head. I stood over him, humming with magic, my rage finally subsiding enough my demon reached out with a large measure of satisfaction and helped herself to his power.

Just a portion of it. I had no idea how she knew the amount to take, but the moment she did, the shields fell and I was free.

Mobicandron groaned as the support behind him collapsed, passing out on the stone. Two demons rushed forward and lifted him with more power, floating him away, though neither of them seemed very happy with their task.

I really didn't give a crap. Not when I was too busy feeling my demon swell like a goddess inside me. She roared her joy, the sound bursting from my own throat and mouth, echoing around the chamber. No one seemed surprised by my outburst so I assumed it was a natural reaction to suddenly having a brand-new flood of fresh magic to fill me up.

Syd. Sassy's mental voice broke through with a hint of panic. *Hurry.*

I glanced out the window, noticed the last of the light had faded. What? I had at least thirty minutes, was sure of it.

Time is different when you're fighting, he sent. *We have to go.*

Dad shoved Meira toward me as Sassy bounded to our feet. "Thank you for dinner," I said directly to Grandmother as I reached for the veil, feeling Dad's power help me, though at the moment I was sure I didn't need him. "It was educational."

She didn't move or say anything as I tore the veil open and headed home.

Tried to.

The thick rubbery membrane fought me, turned from sluggishly cold molasses to a wall of steel. I pounded against it with my power, felt Dad's magic fight beside me, but it was no use.

The legends were true.

Meira and I were trapped on Demonicon.

14

Perhaps it was simply my agitation, but the quarters I found myself pacing in seemed conveniently prepared for me. The huge closet room was full of clothing in my size, the massive bath stocked with bubble baths and scented creams. Maybe I was being paranoid, but knowing now the political maneuverings that went on here, I could only assume my sister and I being trapped was part of some grand plan.

And yet, it was possible, I supposed, these quarters were simply for guests. Since they knew I was coming, and had a wardrobe for me anyway, didn't they need a place to keep it? I wished I could just talk myself into believing it.

If my grandmother had anything to do with our present situation, she'd be hearing from me, Ruler or no Ruler.

An ornately carved side door of black wood swung open and Meira bounced through, Dad and Sassafras trailing along behind her. At least we were adjoining so I could be close to her.

"I love my room!" Meira planted herself on the end of my bed, amber eyes full of happiness.

She was kidding, right?

"Don't get comfortable," I said. She stuck her tongue out at me as I turned my attention to Dad. "So now what?"

He looked as tense as I felt. "We'll wait for morning," he grunted, "and try again. It's possible it's simply that easy." Why then did he sound like he wasn't holding out much hope? "In the meantime, I've been in contact with Theridialis. He's looking into it himself."

I trusted Sassy's dad to have our best interests at heart, so I nodded and drew a deep breath in an effort to calm down. Actually, I was amazed at my own restraint. I hadn't thrown anything or hurtled fireballs at anyone yet.

For the hundredth time, I tested the veil, feeling it as cold and impenetrable as ever. Maybe Dad was right and darkness had some kind of effect on it? But that made no sense to me. I'd ridden the veil many times when the sun was down and never felt anything like this. And if we couldn't go back...

"What about Mom?" She and Gram would be in full lather by now.

Dad winced, crossing his arms over his chest almost as

if for protection. "I crossed to tell them what happened," he said.

"Wait, you can cross?" I scowled at him, trying to process. "And we can't? Why?"

"My effigy," he said softly, as if trying to soothe an angry animal before said animal went into a flip-out rage. Yeah, close one. "My connection to your plane is through my statue. You two don't have anything like that to bring you through. Though it still frustrates me. You're not from this plane. You should be able to go home." His scowl matched mine a moment.

"So what did Mom and Gram say?" I needed to change the subject, if only to break the mood I was sinking into. Any word of home might help.

Dad's frown turned to a wince. "They weren't happy."

I snorted, more tension leaving me, a little smile rising without my permission as I winked at Meira who winked back.

"Tear you a new one, Dad?"

My sister giggled behind her hands while Sassafras leaped up beside her.

Dad sighed. "We'll get this figured out," he said. "I'm sorry, girls. I should never have given in to my mother."

"Nonsense," Sassafras cut in. "You did what you had to.

You know she would have found a way to bring them over herself if it came to it. Ahbi is very determined when she wants something."

Dad nodded slowly, face creased into a frown. When he met my gaze, there was fear in his eyes.

"Just be cautious," he said. Yeah, yeah. Be careful. So sick of hearing him say it by now it made my stomach churn. "I want you to stay in your rooms tonight. You should be safe here."

Like I was planning to wander off. "I can take care of myself, Dad," I said.

"Me too," Meira piped in.

"Clearly," Sassafras stopped grooming one paw to fix me with a disdainful stare. "Like that horrendously pathetic disaster you called a challenge battle?"

It wasn't that bad. "I won, didn't I?"

"Barely." He went back to the meticulous cleaning of his silver fur.

Smartass cat.

"Besides," he went on, "we all know this was Ahbi's original intention."

Harry looked a little guilty. "She assured me—"

It was Sassy's turn to snort. "Since when did your mother ever keep her promises, especially when her own goals were at stake?" He dropped the offending paw and lifted the other to give it the attention it required. "I knew from the moment you told the girls where they were going they wouldn't be heading home right away."

"So why did you let us come?" I wanted to shake his fat little fur body, temper snapping inside me.

Again he met my gaze. "And you would have listened to me. Of course. My bad."

I was seriously considering heaving him out the open window. Just to test the shields around it.

Yeah, right.

Dad's shoulders slumped. "I've been a fool," he whispered. "As I have been all along. There were times I thought I could resist her." When he looked up, his sad face pulled me like a magnet and I wasn't the only one. Meira and I both ran to hug him, his strong arms going around us. "I won't let anything happen to you. I swear it."

"You don't have much of a say in the matter." Sassafras finally gave up his grooming and glared at the three of us from his perch on the bed. "You're stuck here, for as long as it takes to find a way to get you home. But you can't stay cooped up in these quarters."

"What are you suggesting?" Dad's grip tightened on me.

"That I train them to fight." Sassy's fluffy tail whipped

around to coil at his feet, eyes narrowing to slits. "That we show Ahbi and the rest of the family just what the Hayles are made of." He huffed a soft breath. "You know she won't rest until she gets what she wants. So let's give it to her."

Dad was already shaking his head. "This is insane," he said. "I won't allow it."

I pulled away, Meira copying me, reaching for my hand. We stood to face him, united.

"Sassy's right," I said even as a quiver of fear slid down my spine. "Grandmother is after something. Maybe it's me beside her." Not going to happen. "Or maybe she's just testing us to see if we're worthy or something." Stupid, in my opinion. I hated the thought of being a trained dog for her amusement. Not to mention the family's. "But whatever the reason, we're stuck here and I refuse to hide behind you or anyone else."

Tell him, Syd, while cringing inside with the need to have Daddy keep you safe.

Meira's hand tightened on mine. "We're Hayle witches," she said. "And demon royalty." She looked up at me with a wicked grin. "I'd love to show them what that means."

Fear slid away, a bit of excitement taking its place. I'd spent my whole life hiding my magic outside of the family. For once, we were in a place where using power was common and expected. The idea I could actually toss some magic around without worrying about it was kind of appealing.

And even though I'd made a mess of the battle earlier, I'd learned some things. Was pretty sure I could handle myself, especially if Sassy taught me what he knew. The idea of fighting back, of letting my temper out, seemed like a good thing.

Dad must have seen the shift in me—written all over my face—because he shook his head with a laugh and hugged us both again.

"My amazing, willful, powerful daughters," he whispered. "Mother has no idea what she's turned loose."

We all laughed. Until Sassafras broke our mood.

"If you're through patting yourselves on the back," he said, "perhaps you'd like to discuss strategy. And survival."

That cooled me off. "This might be a moot point," I said. "If we're able to cross in the morning."

He didn't seem all that optimistic. "Fine," he said. "Get some sleep. If I'm wrong and you're able to return home tomorrow, we'll never discuss this again. But," he hopped down from my bed, sashaying his way to Meira's room, "when I'm right and you're as stuck here as you have been all along, I'll be waiting."

"That's hardly fair, Sass." He paused and turned when my anger rose to snap at him.

"Fair?" He glared at me as though I'd mortally insulted him. "Throw out the word *fair*, Syd. Oh, and while you're at it? Toss *honest*." He paced back toward me, suddenly a dangerous and menacing presence despite his fluffy silver body. I actually felt my demon clench herself, as though prepared to fight him off, as he stopped at my feet, power radiating out from him. "Integrity. Friendship. Loyalty." His eyes briefly flickered to Dad. "Am I missing any, Harry?"

"Family," Dad said.

Sassy laughed, but there was no humor in the sound. "Ah yes, *family*." He shook himself, fur puffing up. "You have to adjust and do it quickly. New vocabulary: Self-interest. Distrust. Conspiracy."

The hard ball of tension in my stomach started to hurt.

"Got it," I said while Meira's hand tightened in mine, her fear reaching me through our contact.

"No," Sassy snapped, "you don't, Syd. Neither of you do." He swatted at my foot, tail thrashing. "I know you very well. Practically raised the two of you. Neither of you has the instincts you need to survive here."

Not sure if that was an insult or a compliment.

"Sassafras." Dad's frown was enough to tell me he thought the demon cat crossed a line. "Enough."

"I'm not done." He continued to glare at me and I met him in the middle. "Sydlynn, you must be on alert at all times, focused, ready for battle. I don't care about your showmanship at this point." He shook his furry head. "I don't care how ugly your fighting style. As long as you win. But there's only one way you can do so. By attacking first."

"I can handle it," I said. "I hesitated because it was my first time. I know what to expect now."

Sassy sighed. "You have no idea," he said. "Above all, you must be ruthless."

I struggled with my demon as she snarled her agreement. "What do you mean, ruthless?"

"No matter what they say, no matter what happens, how much pain you're causing your opponent, you have to take him out." Sassy's tail twitched as his amber eyes flashed fire. "Do you understand? It's not enough to win, you have to kick him when he's down."

"What is wrong with you people?" I shuddered, hugging myself, Meira pressing into my side as we both finally understood. "I'll fight and I'll win, but I'm not a bully."

"You have to learn to be," Sassy said. "Or they will take advantage of your weakness and you'll fail."

"I can't." I shook my head. "I always swore I'd never be a bully, Sass. And I don't plan on becoming one to satisfy my grandmother and this screwed-up place."

He grunted softly, tail now thrashing. "Fine," he said. "Then when you've finally fallen, stripped to the lowest plane, and they go after your sister," Sass practically spit the word out, "you can explain to Meira why you threw her to the wolves."

Gulp.

"I can do ruthless," I said.

15

Sleeping wasn't an option. Every time I lay down on the bed my head started spinning with so much information the only way I could quiet it was to rise and pace around the room. At least the pajamas I'd dug out of the closet the size of my bedroom at home were kind of normal. Some kind of black silky stuff that felt like I wasn't wearing anything. A little freaky, but the full-length pants and long-sleeved button up shirt looked so much like normal clothes I couldn't resist them.

When someone knocked on my door, I lurched to answer it just to shake myself out of the constant whirl of my thoughts. It wasn't until I had the door half jerked open I realized I should have been more cautious.

Saved by the aide. No battle-seeking relative on the other side to worry about, just Pagomaris, dressed in a long black robe of her own, a smile plastered on her face. She was no longer wearing the giant platform boots she'd forced me into all day and I was surprised to note she was actually shorter than I was.

"Your Highness," she bowed deeply to me. "Ruler would like to see you." When she straightened, there was so much pleading in her face I felt terrible for her. I certainly wouldn't want to work for my grandmother, from what I'd learned so far anyway, nor for anyone else in the family.

I knew Sassafras would be furious with me, Dad too, but I couldn't stand staying cooped up any longer. Besides, it was the middle of the night and I was on my way to see my grandmother. Surely no one would be lurking around—or risk her displeasure if I was late arriving.

"Of course." I closed the door behind me and followed the suddenly fawning Pagomaris out into the hall.

"Excellent, thank you, Highness," she said. "This way, Highness."

Okay, her new attitude was getting old very fast. Clearly she'd expected me to turn her down and was dreading going back to tell Grandmother I wasn't coming.

Then again, maybe I could use Pagomaris's extreme gratitude to my advantage.

"She could have just summoned me." I slowed my pace, forcing her to as well.

"Oh, no," Pagomaris said with a look telling me I'd just suggested sacrilege. "Mental communication is frowned on in the higher planes." I guessed frowned on was an understatement. Which meant Sassy was taking risks when he spoke to me.

Interesting.

I was about to ask her why when the truth hit me. No one trusted anyone else. Touching the mind of another meant a certain level of exposure. Yes, it was possible to shield unwanted thoughts, but it was simple for the connection to be exploited.

Even more interesting. And definitely an advantage if we could keep it in the down-low.

Speaking of which. Um, whom.

Where are you? Sassafras's panicked tone told me volumes. I caught a flash of an image, his view of my room, my bed rumpled, but empty.

Grandmother sent for me. I showed him my own location and felt him swat at me in rage.

You idiot, he snapped. *What were you thinking?*

You would rather she sent guards to drag me in chains? I tried for cold and logical and succeeded not too badly. Enough at least Sassafras's temper eased.

Be on absolute alert, he sent. *I'm staying with your sister. If you need me... oh, Syd.* His mind hugged me fast and hard, the fear behind his anger showing. *Don't do anything stupid.*

He cut off, leaving me shivering, and I almost ran into Pagomaris's back from the distraction of our conversation.

Her smile was as wide as ever as she gestured at the large double doors flanked by two huge guards. "Enjoy your visit," she said before turning and scurrying off.

Abandoning me outside my grandmother's door. Was there more to this invitation than I knew of? Um, duh, Syd.

Time to take Sassy's advice and pay attention.

I doubled up on my shielding, feeling my demon writhe and churn inside me as she prepared for the worst. The guards ignored me as I stepped up to the massive entry, both panels thick with carvings, as high as I was tall twice over, large metal handles in the shapes of screaming demon's faces.

Pleasant.

I raised my hand to knock only to feel power slide through the doors as the handles turned on their own and both swung inward.

Creepy. But a little magic show wasn't going to shake my resolve to stand up to my grandmother.

A wide entry greeted me, opening into the biggest bedroom I'd ever seen. If it could be called that. Full of statues, a hearth the size of a tractor-trailer, two massive desks covered in what looked like paperwork, sofas, chairs... the bed was stuck off in one corner, giant in its own right but dwarfed by the size of the room.

All black décor, all the time, aside from the occasional gold accent. It might have been opulent, but I'd never seen anything so freaking dreary. If I had to live here, I'd be depressed in about a minute.

Everything went away when Grandmother rose from one of the desks and faced me. "Sydlynhamitra," she said in her deep voice. "Welcome."

I was surprised she was alone, fully expecting a small army of attendants to show up at any second, making me pause at the top of the three steps leading down into her quarters. "Grandmother."

That made her smile. Okay then.

She gestured, coming out from behind her desk, dressed in a simple black robe of what looked like the same fabric I wore. Her muscular arms were bare, biceps flexing as she motioned for me to join her. She looked like some old-fashioned female body-builder who refused to let time take away her Miss Universe title. Honestly, I was a little in awe—okay, a lot in awe—of her and found myself stumbling down the first step.

Did I mention how much I love my demon? She caught

me, steadied us, pushed me forward with confidence to join my grandmother where she stood next to the fireplace and a comfortable looking seating area arranged before it.

Fire crackled with power in the deep cavern of the hearth, the scent of smoke only faint as magic or engineering swept the climbing cloud away.

Grandmother towered over me, much like Dad did, and I wondered if he got his physique from her. So funny, I'd always assumed he would look like his own father. Showed what I knew. And while I was still guarded, the smile in her eyes was genuine and I felt my demon relaxing somewhat, though neither of us was willing to release our hold on the shields I'd reinforced.

Don't trust her. Sassy's mental tone was very faint and I could only imagine Grandmother's quarters were warded against power use. *Ever.*

When she reached for me, I took her hand, feeling the heat of her skin, the firm grip of her touch. She guided me to sit next to her on a wide sofa, turning to face me. The pressure of her power was almost more than I could handle, making me grateful for the shields. Refusing to be intimidated, I added strength to them and raised my chin.

She laughed. Did she know what I was feeling? Likely. But I hadn't pissed her off yet, so I figured it was so far, so good.

"Some nectar?" Grandmother poured from a large pitcher, filling two shining goblets with the familiar drink. I'd had some with Theridialis when I'd come across the first time and craved it ever since. My demon's desire made my mouth water and, though drinking it had to be a bad idea, I took the offered cup from my grandmother's waiting hands and let the warmth of the liquid inside the mug heat my hands.

Grandmother sat back with her own, eyes never leaving me. "I've been looking forward to meeting you, my dear," she said. "Your father speaks very highly of you."

The scent of the nectar, that mix of honey and chocolate and pure deliciousness reached my nose, making it twitch. Fine, one sip.

Yummers to the gazillionth power. I felt myself relax a little as the stuff settled in my happy tummy.

"He should talk," I said. "He's pretty amazing himself."

"I understand it was you who returned him home." She didn't move, just watched me, and for the first time I felt the predator in her. So, the open smile was a mask. I was seeing the real Ahbi behind the welcoming grandmother. Good to know.

"No," I said. "That was Sassafras."

"Indeed," she said. "But it was a clever insight on your part that made it possible."

The crystal. How did she know about it? There was no way Dad would have told his family about it, the sorcerer's crystal I'd taken from the evil Demetrius Strong after he'd stolen my demon. The power of that crystal had been enough to transform Dad's statue into indestructible diamond and given Sassy's sacrifice of his life the push it needed to send Dad home.

"Dad and Sass managed it," I said. Wanted to say more. Felt my tongue tingle with the need to keep speaking, but I held back, sipping at the nectar even as my mind begged me to spill everything.

What was wrong with me?

Don't be an idiot, Sassy sent. *Stop drinking that crap.*

The nectar. Oh hell no. I felt the glass slip in my hand as the shock of understanding flexed my muscles for me. I set it firmly aside and noted the flicker of annoyance in Grandmother's eyes before she discarded her own with a thump.

End round one. Ding ding.

What followed was an intense question period that left me shaky and sweating a little. Not that my grandmother asked me anything I would deem a touchy subject, as in things I'd be unwilling to answer, but they were deeply personal in a way, questions about my life at home, my friends and the coven. I was more stressed out I might let something slip I shouldn't than I was about the actual interrogation itself.

"Your mother left you to rule your coven at a very young age," Grandmother said. "How are you coping?"

Zing. "No problems," I said, struggling to keep the ice from my voice.

"Ah yes," she went on, eyes narrowing slightly. "You have your human grandmother to watch over you."

Double zing with a punch to the gut for good measure. "Gram and I co-lead," I said. "Much like you and Vandelarius."

From the twitch of her lips, I finally scored.

But my tally against her didn't get to rise very far. It was an interrogation, no question, hidden behind her smooth, deep voice and her guise as my caring grandparent. There were moments when interest lit her up, times my responses made her close off and ponder before she dove at me with another question.

I have no idea how long it took, but I was grateful when she finally sat forward and stood.

"I've enjoyed our visit," she said. "Perhaps you'd like to get some rest now."

A dismissal if ever I'd heard one. I hadn't had anything

from Sassafras in a while and could only assume Grandmother figured out what he was doing and cut him off. I reached for him, felt an impenetrable wall in my way and knew I was right.

I paused at the door, unsure. I had no idea what awaited me on the other side. Instead of just leaving, I turned back and faced Grandmother.

"It was nice to finally meet you," I said.

Her eyebrows arched slightly. "Good night, Sydlynhamitra," she said.

I drew a breath, tightened my hold on my power and strode out as if I owned the place.

And almost ran right into Sassafras and Meira waiting on the other side.

"What are you two doing here?" I scowled at Sass while my sister pushed past me.

"Grandmother wanted to see me," she said before disappearing through the doors. I turned to go after her only to have them thud shut with finality in my face.

Rude.

Angry did not begin to describe how I felt as I paced the next hour or so away outside Grandmother's doors. Worry for Meira and stress over the whole mess we were in didn't help much. Neither did Sassy's total silence as he glared at the entry. I reached for him at one point and felt his entire focus sharpened to a fine point, aimed directly at the power surrounding the chambers beyond.

No wonder he was so focused.

Eavesdropping was intense business.

But when I tried to insert myself into the subterfuge, he slashed at me with a snarl before refocusing himself.

Jeeze, everyone was being nasty tonight.

When the doors finally cracked open and Meira emerged, I had a tension headache the size of a watermelon banging its way around inside my head, looking for a way out. But she was grinning, bent to lift Sassy into her arms and hug him, smiling at me like everything was okay so I let myself relax as she took my hand and turned me toward our quarters.

"Did you drink it?" Sassy met her eyes.

"No," she said. "Just pretended to like you said."

The nectar. "Nice of you to warn me about it," I groused.

"I didn't think you'd be wandering off in the middle of the night," he snapped back.

"What is it?" The thought brought the yearning back and I had to shut my demon's desire down quickly.

"Nectar has it uses," Sassy said, the grudging tone of his voice making me wonder what kind of history he had with it. "As a mild narcotic, it can boost power and help the user work past certain limitations." That was nicely vague. But he was continuing so I filed further questions away for later. "The problem is, it tends to make the demon more pliable. Willing to speak what shouldn't be spoken." He glared at me, but his expression softened. "You did very well."

"Thanks." I hugged myself as we walked, hating how wound up I was. "Nice of her to drug me."

"She just wants to get to know us." Meira's fingers squeezed mine. "I like her."

Uh-oh. "Meems, she's manipulating us."

She shrugged. "I know," my infinitely wise little sister little sister said. "But once you get past that, she's really nice."

Even Sassafras laughed at that. A laugh choked off in a hiss. I looked up, startled, distracted. Just like he'd warned me not to be.

Didn't look like the demon blocking our path had the same problem.

16

"Sydlynhamitra," she said in a voice echoing through the hallway, "I, Phatshepeset, Lady of the Eighth Plane, challenge you for status."

Nice name. But I wasn't contemplating what she was called or what her ranking was. For once I did as I was told and acted.

Acting I could actually handle. The second she stopped speaking my power was on the move, lashing at her legs in slicing blades of amber fire. It should have worked. I had the jump on her, the shields surrounding her should have been in a nasty puddle at her feet.

Damn it.

I had so much to learn.

Her magic skipped around the edges of mine, forming ripples diffusing the slashing attack until I might as well have come at her with a knitting needle. I barely—barely—had time to dodge aside as her own magic slid forward, a hissing snake, to strike at me with venom

I was certain would do more damage than I was willing to take.

Any damage was unacceptable, to be honest.

My demon roared her fury, splitting our magic in two down the middle, arms of force striking outward, coming together around her with so much pressure I felt my ears pop as the magic whooshed around her shields.

Her magic slithered, shimmering and shuddering, the constant motion making it impossible to crush her as she eddied and flowed like water, my demon unable to get a grip on her at all.

Syd! Sassy's voice broke through my intense concentration. *Stop trying to beat her with a club and use your head!*

My head? He actually expected me to have time to think? A dozen of her magic snakes oozed around my feet, striking over and over at my shields, sending pin-pricks of pain through me with every blow until my demon snarled her frustration.

Okay, think, Syd. She's slippery. What works against something that you can't hold onto? I had to figure out a way to pin her down, but how?

I need to find out how to stick to her in order to get a grip. Stick.

Ow! DAMN IT, that HURT! A large version of her little

snakes took a giant bite out of the side of my shield forcing me to patch it while another took a second bite out of the other side.

Nononononono. I couldn't lose. Couldn't.

Sand. As I spun and blocked the snakes, on the panicked defensive, I had an image of being at the beach, covered in suntan oil. And how the sand would stick—

Not thinking, refusing to second-guess myself as a third snake tore a slice out of my shields, making me stagger to one knee, I gathered my power and flung it at her.

But not to pound away at her. Not at all. As it traveled outward it broke up into small pieces, fracturing further and further until it shimmered in the air like glitter. Phatshepeset's smile of derision faded as she batted at it. But the dust of my power settled on her, around her, sinking into the undulation of her shields, like sand settling to the bottom of the ocean.

I staggered to my feet as her snakes disappeared, watched for a moment as she writhed and struggled, slapping at herself where the pin-points of magic touched her as they slid through her wards and settled on her body.

What are you waiting for? Sassy's snapped command broke through my daze. *Finish her.*

Right. I called to my power and drew it together,

cocooning her inside her own wards. With my teeth gritted, I jerked my outstretched hand into a fist, crushing her under the weight of my now solid magic.

Phatshepeset cried out in agony, collapsing to the ground as I then opened my hand wide, shattering her shields outward, sending the shards flying to dissipate in little puffs of gold.

My demon snarled as she shoved me forward, siphoning off a measure of the girl's magic. It slid inside us, the reptile feel of it integrating with my power while the rush of extra energy sent goose bumps racing over my skin.

Satisfied, my demon gave me back control. Sick and a little horrified, I stood over the fallen demon girl who stared at me with terror in her eyes before limping to her feet and scuttling away.

"Ruthless," Sassy said. "Well done."

I turned on him with a snarl. "Shut the hell up." I stomped off to my room, throwing the doors open, not caring if he and Meira followed.

They did, of course.

"I don't know why you're angry," Sassy said. "You knew what was coming."

"It's this damned place." I spun, letting my frustration out, while Meira watched me with sadness on her face.

"How can people live like this? What the hell is wrong with them that they can just treat each other like fresh meat?" I couldn't wait to go home and forget Demonicon ever existed.

Sassy ignored what I said. "Had you some training, you would have seen through her attack style and taken her out easily."

"I said shut it," I snapped. "Besides, it's almost morning. I just want to get the hell out of here." Hope, thin and fragile. It had to work.

It just *had* to.

I spent the rest of the night perched on the end of the bed with Sassy on one side and Meira on the other. Enough rummaging in my closet had turned up the clothes I arrived in and I'd changed, ready and waiting to leave this insanity behind me.

Dad found us there, Meira wilting against my side, just after sunrise. He didn't comment, though I could tell from the pinched look on his face he knew not only about our visit to see Grandmother, but had also heard about the fight.

"Time to get you girls home," he said, "before anything else happens."

Yup. He'd heard all right.

I stood up, drew a breath. "Right then." I reached for the veil and, for a moment, felt the hope I'd harbored rise and swell. The spongy, rubber-like consistency of the veil was back.

Wicked.

Except no matter how hard I tried, Dad's power and Sassy's tied to mine, I couldn't get the damned thing to part. There were brief moments where I thought I might win through, when I could feel the edge of home, but the veil simply folded back in and pushed me aside.

Panting and frustrated, I finally jerked free, not willing to admit defeat, but with no idea what to do next.

Dad hugged me. "I'm sorry, honey."

Fury surged. Where was he last night when I was being interrogated by his mother? And attacked by one of his family? The anger faded quickly. This wasn't Dad's fault.

Nope. I blamed Grandmother.

"Enough," Sassy snapped. "You can whine and cry later. Right now you both have training to do and so help me, if either of you gives me a moment of trouble, I'm going to show you why I was the best demon challenger ever born."

First order of business made me actually uncomfortable and kind of anxious at the same time. Sassafras led me into my ginormous closet and proceeded to choose an outfit for me, something he deemed suitable for whatever he had in mind. Not that I was normally shy around him, but having my demon cat pick my wardrobe was more than a little weird and kind of creepy.

"Oh stop it," he snapped as I hid a nervous giggle behind my hand as his magic pulled down a large wrap-like coat and dropped it at my feet. "Grow up, would you, please?"

Done with me, he waddled out to badger my sister, leaving me to dress in the floor-length flowing pant things and short, tight top baring my midriff, more of the stupid platform boots and the lightweight wrap he'd chosen. All blue this time. I felt like I'd had a very bad accident with a magic marker.

But worse than the clothes? Imagine my shock when

Sassafras led Meira and I out of our quarters and to the elevator.

"Aren't we supposed to be training?" I clenched my jaw against the rising vista below us as the platform dropped about fifty feet before coming to a halt again. I didn't think I'd ever get used to it.

"Just trust me, for once in your life." He sounded so snippy I let it go, knowing his concern for us was testing his temper as much as mine.

We emerged not into a hall or a large chamber, but overlooking what seemed to be some kind of arena. Bleacher seats, though far more grandiose and comfortable than any stadium I'd ever seen, rose above a large stone opening where a number of demons seemed to be doing battle.

"Training ground," Sassafras said, eyes locked on the scene below as we walked down the wide stairs to the bottom. There was a wistful quality to him suddenly that made me want to stroke his fur and comfort him. After all, hadn't he himself spent years—decades as far as I knew— in this very arena training to fight for status?

"I still think it would be easier to just train in our quarters." I felt the hum of magic as we finally touched down on the arena floor and understood why we were here even as Sassafras's snippy voice filled me in.

"Unless you're prepared to expend enough energy to shield your rooms," he said at his most haughty, "you'll use the training ground like everyone else."

He didn't have to be such a jerk about it.

Besides, he sent in a tightly closed thread, *this way you are able to witness some of your competition in action. How many times do I have to tell you to pay attention?*

I was seriously going to throttle his ass. Once we were home, safe and sound.

Right now, it seemed, I needed him.

More than a little sour over the whole thing, I followed Sass and Meira to the center of the open area. When he stopped in the middle and turned to face us, I hesitated. Every eye was locked on us, the rest of the combatants lining the walls of the round arena.

Way to make us stand out like sore thumbs, Sass. I didn't need the extra pressure. They'd be watching anyway, but it would have been nice to have a wall at my back just in case. What was he thinking?

You're going to stand out no matter what we do, he sent. *Might as well make yourselves easy to observe.*

Easy targets you mean. I shifted nervously, trying to watch all of the other demons at once.

Don't be ridiculous, he sent. *The arena is off limits to status*

*matches. Training only. Anyone who breaks the rule is stripped
and tossed out of the city. The law has stood for generations.
Now focus.*

Sassafras had always been a bossy-pants, but his new
attitude was really rankling. I knew he was worried, that
he just wanted to help. And was likely the only one who
could help. But I'd survived two fights already and didn't
think being talked to like a baby was warranted.

Like Sassafras gave a crap what I thought.

Typical.

I thought fighting was hard work. What Sass put us
through in the next several hours left me even more wrung
out than trying to keep from telling my grandmother
what she wanted to know. With his power snapping like
a whip, Sass put Meira and me through our paces as if
we were prized thoroughbreds who hadn't been working
at potential.

From shielding to slashing to mustering fire, shredding
and the slippery nature of my previous evening's attacker,
I struggled to keep up. Meira, on the other hand, took to
his teaching like she was only remembering things she'd
forgotten, often laughing when the magic she needed slid
easily into place.

You're fighting your demon, Sass snapped at last. *You're accustomed to being in the driver's seat. Let her take the pressure, do the work. You guide her.*

My demon rumbled her approval so I gave it a go. Turned out he was right.

Again.

Ack.

I looked up from recoiling a whip of my own made from pure magic, drawing it back slowly rather than allowing it to dissipate, the pressure of holding it intact taking all of my attention. But the moment Sass let me release it at last, I realized we weren't alone.

Not that the two watching us had intruded in any way. But they stood close enough, arms crossed, bodies tilted toward each other while they smirked in our direction, they might as well have.

Cousins, Sassafras sent quickly.

The way the rest of the combatants didn't look our way made me think the guy/girl pair probably possessed impressive status themselves. They looked about my age, him tall and broad, typical demon physique with bulging biceps and a wide jaw. She was almost as tall as he was but slender, though her muscles rippled under her thin clothing. They looked enough alike I figured they had to be fairly closely related.

"Nicely done, cousin." The girl's voice cut with an edge though her words said otherwise. "I've never seen a fire whip used quite like that."

Her companion, probably her brother, snickered.

"Tanasharia." Sassy's tone was flat and bored. "You haven't grown. What a surprise."

She snarled at him immediately. "I wasn't speaking to you, damned one." Tanasharia tossed her head, long black hair whipping around her like a weapon. Her eyes locked on mine again. "I was thinking we could have a friendly spar. Flex our power."

"No." Sassafras stepped in front of me, his small cat body no match for her physically, but the pressure of his power shoving her back a step. "You know the rules, Duchess."

She didn't argue or even look at him, just shrugged. "If you change your mind," she said, "I'd be happy to show you how things work around here."

The pair turned and wandered off, the other demons in the arena bowing and acting all reverential.

"Okay," I said, "who were the douchebags?"

Sassy sighed. "Tanasharia, Duchess of the Third Plane and Cypherion, her brother, Prince of the Second Plane." He looked up into my eyes, his guarded and flashing fire. "Yes," he said, "the Cypherion your father mentioned, heir to the Second Seat."

Vandelarius's kids. Nice.

"Don't underestimate them," Sassy said. "They may not have changed since I fought them, they may still be arrogant and think more highly of themselves than they should, but they are powerful and known to cheat if they think they can get away with it."

"Which they can," I said, "because of who they are."

Sassy's cat-shrug made his fur ripple. "Don't get me wrong," he said. "Cheating, no matter who you are, will get you in serious trouble." He paused and I wondered if he was thinking about himself. "But a certain amount of… creative fighting goes on, and as long as you don't cross certain lines, no one will turn you in."

"Such as?" I needed all the help I could get.

"Forget it." Sassy's snarl told me I'd crossed one of his lines. "Focus on skills. Then when you're even remotely close enough to getting it right, we'll talk about it." He snorted. "My luck you'd overdo it on the first go and end up powerless and an outcast."

"Should we worry about those two coming after us?" Meira looked like she wanted to take them both on with her bare hands, right here, right now. Made me feel much better about her chances.

"No," he said. "Not yet. They're probably waiting to see

what you'll do, sizing you up. I've fought them both, defeated them both. Mind you, that was a long time ago. But neither feels all that much more powerful than they used to." He swiped one paw over his whiskers. "Would be just like those two to run on their reputations and lose their fighting skills."

Well, that could be helpful.

"The worst part is they've always been your grandmother's favorites." Sass let his paw drop. "And they will see the two of you as a threat to their position."

"So who do you think will come at us next?" I'd fought a knight and a lady so far, Tenth and Eighth planes. I winced inwardly as I realized how far I still had to go to reach my dear, dear cousins.

"I don't know," he admitted. "I've been out of the game for too long. But you'll mainly face the family, so at least I can find out. Tanasharia and Cypherion confirmed that much for me at least."

He stood up and flicked his tail at me. "You two keep practicing," he said. "Don't leave until I come back for you."

Sass scampered off, but I reached for him before he leaped to the top step. *Where are you going?* Way to abandon us to the wolves.

To do some research, he sent before he vanished through the exit with a flick of silver fur.

18

I felt like a bit of an idiot training without Sassafras, doing the same stuff over and over again, but I had to admit, by the time he trotted down the stairs to join us again, I was feeling a lot more confident about what I'd learned.

He made Meira and I go through our paces, one at a time, praising my sister while his snarky tone told me he wasn't completely happy with my progress.

Maybe he shouldn't have just left us, then, hmmm?

The moment we set foot outside the training ground I was accosted by another cousin. At least Calanothalmunon was only a Knight of the Fifteenth Plane. Considering I'd spent the afternoon practicing, his timing was unfortunate.

Sassy didn't have a negative thing to say as I swiftly countered the demon's attack and, seeing the weakness in the rigid shielding he held, honed my power into a chisel and hammer, shattering his protections around him.

Maybe my easy win and the absorption of Calanothalmunon's power should have made me happy, but instead it made me nothing but cranky.

Made worse when I had to stop and observe two demons fighting each other on the elevator platform. It was weird to be on the outside of a battle but it told me, loud and clear, this was the way things were on Demonicon. Meira and I weren't special in that regard. It was fight and win or lose and be reduced.

When the elevator was cleared, the victor marching off with a big smile on his stupid face, his opponent, dragging himself past us, eyes vicious, I had to sigh. The trip up wasn't so bad, so lost was I in the absolute absurdity of it all. I think I was ready for another when a girl confronted me two steps from my quarters.

I sent her packing, her shielding in tattered strips hanging from her, power now mine, mollified to see the furious look on Meira's face. Someone cared I was being treated like a punching bag.

Yeah, not quite. Seemed my little sister had her own reasons for being miffed.

As the girl demon whose mouthful of a name I'd already forgotten ran off, Meira pouted.

"Where's my battle?"

Oh. My. Swearword.

She glared at me as I laughed my way into my quarters, but I just couldn't help myself.

"Bloodthirsty." Sassy head-butted her leg. "But it's good, Meira. And don't worry. Your time will come. They will test both of you carefully, with powerful challengers and those who don't stand a chance against you," from the snort he gave he considered my last two opponents in the latter category, "until they understand your fighting styles and can use them against you."

"Way to make us feel better, Sass." I flopped down on the bed, all at once exhausted.

"I'm not here to coddle you, Sydlynn," he said. "My job is to keep you both safe. And winning."

When did pacing become my default stress release? The moment I started moving again the power flooded back into my limbs and my weariness faded. Had to be a side effect of winning. And while I felt powerful all over again, it still drove me to irritation.

"How can demons live like this?" I stopped and faced Sassy who observed me with his calm amber eyes. "In what reality does fighting for your life every five seconds, this non-stop battle for dominance, become normal?"

"I see you need a history lesson," he said, hopping up on

the bed and curling into a ball. "Very well. I suppose it's good for both of you to understand why things are the way they are." Sassy settled his chin on his paws, gaze far away. "You ask why the fighting, why the ritualized battles. Honestly, it's the only way to keep this place from falling apart."

I sank down on the bed beside him, Meira stretching out on her stomach with her chin in her hands, feet bobbing behind her.

"It used to be demons killed each other all the time," Sassy went on. "Devouring each other's energy. Crossing planes to slaughter, pillage, build their power bases and do war only to have their armies decimated by demons more powerful and on higher planes than they."

Awful. Sounded like the Dark Ages.

"The first Ruler rose from the constant battling with the idea if he could assemble the planes together, he could control them all." Sassy's abrupt exhale was amused. "Don't for a moment think Zelmanharitopel's plan was to unify all demonkind for their own good. He did it for purely selfish reasons. But the results were the same."

"It worked," I said, fascinated despite myself. "The planes became one big one." The magic behind something like that boggled my mind.

"They did," Sassy said. "In order to keep the newly

assembled Demonicon together, Zel had to use a lot of fast talking and a really big stick." He chuckled softly. "The royal historians will give you a different account, mind you, but this is the gist. Once he beat his dominance into the rest, he created laws, joined by his number one rival, Bringdalimenaria, gave her what we now call Second Seat and mated with her."

"The first ruling pair." Meira's smile seemed almost dreamy. "This is wicked cool."

Sassy flicked his tail at her. "The law stated no demon was permitted to kill another for their power. Instead, ritualized battles were created in order to facilitate the ebb and flow of magic, called status." He sounded sad again. "There were those who fought the new ways in the beginning, but they were stripped and sent to the lowest planes, the dregs of demonkind. Most saw the benefits of obedience and society began to form, culture to develop where once we had none."

Peace could do that for a people. Or whatever they called their compromise.

"I have to admit," he whispered, nose now covered with his tail, "I'm a little sickened by the whole thing now. I've been away too long." As though he were accusing himself of weakness.

I leaned in and hugged him gently, stroking his ears and the soft fur on the top of his head.

"We're lucky to have you," I said. "They don't deserve you, Sass."

"Nope, they don't," Meira said, kissing him.

"Agreed." We all looked up. How had I missed Dad's entrance? He smiled gently at all of us, though the feel of him was grim. "Why do you think I prefer your home to mine, girls?"

And yet, as we rose to hug our father, I couldn't help but think things really weren't all that different at home. Only our leaders used money and other kinds of power instead of magic.

I wasn't all that surprised to be called on again in the middle of the night. In fact, I was expecting it, already up after a short nap.

Sassafras warned me about the possibility as we dined in private with Dad.

"She's fishing for something," he said of my grandmother. "Don't underestimate her."

"She's a mistress of subtleties," Dad agreed. "You won't know what she's after until she has it from you."

"Just be careful what you say," my demon cat said. "And for goodness sakes, control your temper."

I fell into a short sleep after leaving the others to talk, feeling much more refreshed for a bit of rest despite the fact I should have been exhausted. A long shower in the amazing bathroom, piping hot water pouring from a huge fountain gushing over my body, did wonders for my state of mind.

By the time Pagomaris knocked, I was smiling and ready.

No more hesitation. I strode into Grandmother's presence like I was the one ready to ask questions. Her powerful magic didn't intimidate me this time. What was the worst she could do? I was already trapped here, fighting for my status. It wasn't like she was going to challenge me. Maybe she could make my life miserable, but I was willing to take the chance if it meant keeping my dignity and my head.

She clearly saw the change because her welcome was cooler than the night before. When she sat next to me on the same couch, observing, hands reaching for the nectar, I laughed out loud.

"Just ask me," I said, not sure where my bubbling good humor came from, but willing to let it ride and see where it took me. Maybe I was so past the stupid games I felt I had nothing to lose.

Grandmother's smile was dark and dangerous, but she nodded and began.

This time she pulled nothing, direct and blunt. But she didn't quiz me about home or my other magicks, but about the battles I'd fought and won so far. Why did I choose this particular attack or that specific defense? Was I thinking when I went in this direction or just reacting? How much of a disconnect was there between me and my demon?

That question made me pause. Consider. Laugh again.

"None," I said with total honesty. "We're one."

My demon rumbled her agreement.

By now my happy-go-lucky feelings faded. How did she know anything at all about who I'd been? How Gram's magic kept me from bonding with my demon from birth? Where was Grandmother getting her information? As far as I knew, the only other demon who understood my story was Theridialis.

No way. A traitor? Would he really betray us?

I found myself mentally shaking my head as Grandmother's prying questions went on. It couldn't be. It wasn't like I knew every single demon Dad confided it. It was likely one of them betrayed him. Or, for all I knew, he'd told her himself.

That would be a jackass move, yes. But I couldn't bring myself to believe Theridialis stepped over the line like that. No, I didn't know everything about him, but he'd never given me a reason to doubt his loyalty to Dad.

Besides, Sassy would never forgive him. And from what I could see of their relationship, things were finally mending between father and son. Surely the kindly older demon wouldn't risk his newly minted bond with Sassafras.

When Grandmother asked me why I chose to use the sand attack, I paused. "What would you have done?"

She actually looked startled, the first open and honest expression I'd seen on her face, as though she never once expected me to have the nerve to ask.

Grandmother sat there in silence for a heartbeat or two before nodding. "I would have done as you did," she said, tone grudging, but with a hint of respect I took as a win.

She surged to her feet and, for a moment, I considered remaining where I was. But the tightness around her eyes told me I'd pushed her as far as she was willing to be pushed right then, so I stood and nodded to her in my very best coven leader mode with the small smile Mom reserved for those she had to be nice to.

My expression, my stance, had the desired effect. Grandmother's jaw clenched as she bent over me.

"Sleep well, my dear," she said in a voice rumbling like a waking volcano, her power pushing down on me. In that exact instant I knew her, who she was, why she was and I pushed back.

"You too, Grandmother," I said while the bully inside her backed off.

End round two. Ding freaking ding.

Small victory, really. I watched my sister enter the chamber, paced with Sassafras while Meira had her visit,

It was much shorter this time, though she was smiling when she emerged, and seemed quite happy.

I couldn't begrudge her how she was feeling, not when there seemed to be so little around here to be happy about. Instead, I took her hand and followed my demon cat down the dark stone hall, bare feet making soft sounds on the polished floor.

"What did you talk about?" I was curious enough to ask. After all, Meira didn't have many battles to keep Grandmother interested.

"Nothing really," she said. "Syd, would you ever want to live here?"

That was sudden and absolutely flabbergasting. "Sorry?"

Meira shrugged. "I like it," she said. "Feels like home."

Sassy's tail twitched ahead of us, ears flickering, but that was the only response he gave to her statements. I personally felt a surge of concern and wondered what Grandmother had been telling my sister. Not like Meira was gullible. She'd been through hell and back again too, with the coven and Nicholas DeWinter kidnapping her to use her against Mom back when I lost my demon.

Not your choice, Sassy sent. *It's Meira's decision if she chooses to like it here.*

He was absolutely right.

Didn't make me feel any better, though.

A part of me groaned in annoyance as we rounded the last corner and came face-to-face with a demon blocking our way. He was pretty short, more Meira's height, and seemed young. I felt my irritation twist my face as I crossed my arms over my chest and glared down at him, fully aware as I let him feel the full push of my power I was acting like my grandmother.

"Seriously?" I nudged him. "Go home, squirt."

He scowled at me though his gaze never left my sister. "Hathenemeira," he said, "I am Jarismorthistal, Knight of the Nineteenth Plane and I challenge you for status."

20

Meria was so fast I barely followed her. Within thirty seconds of her first attack, the young demon she fought lay prone on the floor, groaning, while she grinned at me, amber eyes flaring with new power, as if this whole thing was really funny.

I wished I could agree with her.

My heart clenched as she absently strode over her fallen attacker as though he wasn't worth further notice, an arrogant tilt to her head, shoulders back so far I thought she'd crack in half.

"This is too easy," Sassy muttered as we followed her. "You're winning far too quickly for a pair of amateurs."

Meira turned and glared at him, just outside my door. "I kicked his ass!"

My demon agreed with her one hundred percent, but Sassy just swatted at her on the way by, muttering to himself.

I spent the rest of the night in and out of sleep, tossing

and restless, waking from dreams of my sister attacking me while she laughed. Unsettled and twitchy, I met Meira and Sassafras for breakfast, grunting at Dad as I flopped into a chair across from him.

He very intelligently ignored my attitude as he sipped his coffee. Or what passed for coffee on Demonicon. It smelled the same with a dose of cinnamon and some kind of fresh flower thrown in for good measure. "Theridialis wants to see us in the lab," he said. "Up for a road trip?"

It felt like I'd been trapped on the mountain forever. "Absolutely." Funny how the idea of a change of scenery perked me up. Until I remembered our arrival. "Please, no parades."

Dad chuckled, handsome face kind. "No parades," he said. "We'll take the train from the fiftieth level."

"No veil riding?" I sighed in disappointment. "We could be there now."

"You know it's against the rules," Sassy snapped, head lifting from a bowl of white creamy stuff mixed with chunks of meat.

Rules. He didn't want to hear just how sick I was of rules.

At least I didn't have Pagomaris around to dress me in some ridiculous outfit. Obviously, she considered her job done, having delivered us to Grandmother. Aside from our nocturnal journeys to visit Ruler, the anxious and overly smiley aide was nowhere to be found.

Which meant I dressed myself. Three quarters of the outfits in my closet were what I would term so outrageous they weren't really clothes and I had no sweet clue what to do with them even if I did want to try them out. In thirds, the remainder were: Halloween Material, Wouldn't be Caught Dead and I Can Live With It If I Have To.

From the final category I chose a pair of black—I was so sick of black I wanted to scream—pants so tight they squeezed my butt and made it look sexy, actually. Hmm. A sweater thing with gauze, some kind of feathers I could wrench into a shape suiting me and—would wonders never cease—a pair of flattish shoes only two inches platformed, and not bad.

Would do me.

As I emerged into the hall I had to grasp my chest with both hands as I gasped and almost fell back. A whole phalanx of guards—like I knew what a phalanx was, but this had to be it—waited for me, filling the hallway with very large, very intimidating bodies.

I spotted Dad in their midst flanked by Meira and the very annoyed looking Sassafras and moved to join them, keeping my distance from the muscle-bound men and women who stared straight ahead and looked dangerous.

"Um," I said. "What gives?"

Dad rolled his eyes before bending to kiss my cheek. "Escort," he said like he was as irritated as the cat at my feet before turning and pushing his way through them. Well, it looked like he'd have to. But the moment Dad began his motion the guards shifted, making a perfect column of protection around us.

Felt like being guarded by a football team. If said team's members were all about seven feet tall and moved like programmed robots.

The very crowded elevator deposited us at a large station while I tried not to hyperventilate, certain all that weight was going to be too much for the platform to support. I'd not noticed the rail line running from the mountain into the city, probably because I'd done everything I possibly could to not look down. But now I hovered near the edge, a glowing amber shield between me and the long, long drop to the rock below, waiting for the train and wishing I could just ride the damned veil already.

Our transportation came humming along the line toward us from deeper in the city, a long, thin platform, this one contained and with seating ever present. I chose to perch on one of the rather comfortable chairs built into the wall and keep my eyes locked on my feet in an effort not to throw up.

I really had to do something about this phobia when I got home.

The train slowed after a short journey, the only indication we were coming to a halt Sassafras's impatient tail swish. I looked up in surprise to find we'd arrived at another station and had to disembark. Finally on more solid ground on the elevated platform, I recognized Theridialis's tower only a short distance away.

A platform rose and we were herded onto it, before one of the guards activated the console standing at the back and we whipped through the air toward the tower without even a whisper of air passing through the protective shield. I wanted to feel better, knowing the wards were there to keep me from falling, but irrationality won.

Cold sweat sucks.

The platform deposited us on the top level, the same as the lab.

"Wait here," Dad ordered the guards before striding off into the tower. I didn't bother to check and see if the automatons obeyed, but followed him quickly, breathing a sigh of relief when stone closed around me.

"Chicken," Sassy said with a soft clucking sound.

You betcha.

It was clear from the look on Theridialis's face when we strode into the lab his news wasn't good.

"I'm sorry," he said, perched on the edge of his stool, thick hands folded over the round paunch of his middle. "I've tried everything."

"So the girls are trapped." Dad slumped a little.

"That's the thing," Theridialis said, voice testy. "They shouldn't be."

"Sorry?" My dashed hopes gave way to confusion.

"As far as I can tell," Sassy's father said, "there is no reason why you shouldn't be able to go home. You energy is in tune with your home plane. Your power is sufficient to break the barrier between. But for some reason I can't uncover, the veil simply won't part for your physical forms to pass."

"Physical." Dad hesitated. "How about spirits?"

Theridialis looked sad. "Yes, indeed," he said. "That should be possible."

Was he suggesting we cross over and tell my mother goodbye?

"Miriam will want to speak with you," Dad said, confirming my fears. "I can be the catalyst for your crossing at least." He held out his hands to us. Numb, I took his right while Meira took his left. I felt Dad reach for the veil as Sassafras came to perch on Dad's feet.

We crossed over together before I could collect myself, before I could come up with something to say. Too late, my heart in my throat, I felt my spirit leave and slide through the veil, tied to Dad. It was the weirdest sensation, being disembodied, and for a moment I worried I'd lose myself.

The basement looked different, an amber haze over everything. Even Mom seemed softer, more mortal to my view. She paced the pentagram, coming to a sudden halt as we crossed over, a low cry emerging from her throat as she rushed toward us.

Stopped. One hand rose to cover her open mouth, eyes full of tears.

"Harry," she whispered. "What's happening?"

Someone howled, feet thudding on the wooden stairs as Charlotte hurtled herself at me, barreling through me like I wasn't there.

Which I guess I really wasn't. Clinched it for me.

She snarled and tried again, lovely face twisted, wolf in her eyes. She shook all over, hands clawing to reach me.

"Charlotte," I said. "It's okay, Charlotte."

A second pair of feet raced down the stairs, Gram's fluffy

striped socks distinctive before I even caught sight of the rest of her. She approached the weregirl with a frown on her face, though I could see the concern in her eyes when her gaze met mine for a moment.

"Didn't work out the way you expected, did it, Harry?" Gram's arms went around Charlotte.

Dad's grim scowl deepened. "No, Ethpeal," he said. "It didn't."

Mom drew a breath, visibly pulling herself under control, though her hands fisted around large chunks of her velvet skirt as though she needed the contact to keep herself steady. "What's being done to correct this?" All Council Leader, my mother. Not that I blamed her.

Coping mechanisms came in all shapes and sizes.

"We're doing everything we can," Dad said.

"We're okay, Mom." Meira beamed at her. "It's kind of fun. And Grandmother is really nice."

Mom's lips trembled as she smiled at Meira. "That's wonderful, honey," she said.

"You're in danger." Charlotte shook like a leaf, still trying to reach me, madness in her eyes. "All the time, you're in danger."

"I know," I said. "I'm sorry, Charlotte. But I swear I'm winning."

She bobbed her head, swallowed hard. "Come home," she whined, the whimper of a kicked puppy.

Working on that.

"We don't have much time." Dad glanced sideways at me. "But we won't stop until this is over and the girls are home safe. Remember, we thought it was impossible for me to return to my own plane and a way was made."

"Hopefully this time I won't have to die." Sassy's dry wit broke the thin veneer of control Mom held. Her hands covered her face and she sobbed.

I couldn't stand it and was grateful when Dad released his hold on his effigy. The crossing back to Demonicon was almost cleansing, though I struggled with the memory of my mother so distraught, my bodywere being slowly driven to madness.

But the worst was my last vision, the fear in Gram's eyes as if she never expected to see me again.

21

We were a pretty gloomy bunch when we returned to the lab. Theridialis just shook his head slowly, jowls jiggling a little. Dad slumped into a nearby chair while Sassafras circled the room, tail straight up like a flag waving as he made his agitated circuit.

"There has to be a way." Dad stood suddenly, brow low over his eyes. "What haven't we considered?"

"There are more tests I can run." Theridialis didn't seem all that positive, but my need for hope latched onto his words like a lifeline.

Sassafras leaped up on the table, daintily weaving his way through the beakers and jars until he stood across from his father.

"Make me a demon again." He sounded a little out of breath and, to be honest, so was I with that request fresh from his cat mouth.

Theridialis met his son's amber eyes. "What good could that serve?"

"I could fight for the girls." His tail thrashed, knocking over several fragile-looking instruments which I barely caught with my magic. No one else seemed to care or notice so I gently set them on the floor, my power coiling away as Sassy went on. "I know how these things work. If I had a mortal body, I could challenge the cousins myself and keep the girls safe."

Was that desperation in his voice? My confidence plummeted as I realized he didn't think we stood a chance after all, no matter what success we had.

Way to make a girl feel useful.

Theridialis reached out very gently and stroked Sassy's face. The Persian leaned into his father's fingers, a soft purr emerging though his tail didn't quiet.

"My son," the portly scientist said, "if I were able, I would have by now."

Sassafras hissed and pulled away. "Fine," he snapped, turning on us. "Then we have work to do."

Yeah, like I really wanted to put the effort in now I knew what he really thought.

Dad perked, gaze far away for a moment before he shook his head and stood.

"I have to go," he said. "I'm needed at the Seat." Dad hesitated a moment before making a visible decision. "You two stay here and let Theridialis run his tests. I'll leave the guards to bring you back if I don't return myself."

"Harry," Sassy said, "you need your own protection."

Dad turned without arguing with him. "If I'm not back my guards will watch over you."

And he was gone.

"Thought mental communication was frowned on?" I met Sassy's eyes. The cat didn't blink, tail swishing still.

"It is," he growled. "I don't like it one bit."

"Maybe we should just go with Dad." Even Meira, who had been rather upbeat despite the news we were trapped, seemed concerned.

I shrugged and took his stool, trying not to let the sense of defeat win. "Let's just do the tests," I said.

Most of what Theridialis did seemed futile, though I recalled the last batch of testing he'd run me through and none of it made sense either. Meira found the whole process fascinating, asking a ton of questions in an excited chatter while I just did as I was told, lost in my private storm cloud.

"Thank you both." Theridialis examined a set of equations he'd written in the air with amber fire, face creased in a frown of concentration. "I'll examine my findings and perhaps we'll try the crossing again tomorrow."

"Good then." I hopped down from my stool, needing to

move all of a sudden, to shake my melancholia. "Back to the Seat it is."

Meira made a face, but followed me after giving the distracted Theridialis a quick hug. He smiled at her and patted her head like she was very small before muttering to himself, wandering around the lab with his equations floating after him.

Sassafras snorted and led the way to the exit, tip of his tail sagging into a question mark as we approached the elevator and found it empty.

Hmm. Hadn't Dad said he'd leave his guards? No floating vehicle waited. Maybe they were at the bottom.

Sassy hissed. "On our own," he said. "Something isn't right."

I paused, felt around me. I'm not sure what I sought, but at least I didn't come across any obvious threats.

"Well, we can't stay here forever," I said. "Let's go."

Sassy swatted my leg. "We wait for Harry."

I'm not sure where my sudden surge of stubbornness came from. Maybe I was tired of being afraid, or maybe I was just sick of feeling cooped up in the mountain palace. But whatever the case, I slipped around my guardian feline and onto the platform. Meira grinned and joined me, leaving Sassafras to stare at us while we waited for him to come aboard.

"We'll leave without you," I said, not really sure if I meant it.

He must have believed me because, grumbling and muttering, he came on board just as the elevator began to drop.

It deposited us on the street, out in the open. I'd been here before, guided to a platform surrounded by guards and dressed in a ghastly outfit. This time there was no cordon, no gathered crowd. Just normal demons going about their normal business on the cobbled streets of their city.

Fear spiked for a moment until I realized for the first time we were totally anonymous. No one knew we were here or who we were. I didn't know how likely it was any cousins would be in the area, but I hoped not. This could finally be an opportunity to have a look around.

"The train," Sassy said. "Is that way." He motioned with his head. "Don't get any ideas."

Meira giggled and scooped him up. "We'll get to the train," she said, winking at me, "when we've done a little snooping."

Sassy's grumbling was lost in her laughter as she turned and headed down the street in the opposite direction.

Now, I totally understood his concern. We were strangers in this place, with what amounted to a bounty on our heads if any of our cousins caught up with us. And yet, for the first time since we arrived, I felt like a normal person again. Okay, demon. But the point is, as I strolled behind my sister and the arguing silver Persian in her arms to the end of the street and into what turned out to be a giant open-air market, I found myself smiling and actually enjoying myself.

Considering where we'd just come from and the reality of what might be our future, I'd take a few minutes distraction in a crowd where no one knew well enough to challenge me for status.

That whole thing was going to get old fast if I had to put up with it for long.

Meira squealed in delight over some hand-made jewelry and what looked like clothing knit with metal while I let her have her fun, keeping an eye out just in case, though Sassafras seemed to have the guardian market cornered, his paws over her shoulder, cat eyes everywhere at once.

It wasn't until my sister backed away with a sad look on her face I realized we didn't have any money.

"Sorry, Meems," I said. "We'll get some cash from Dad and come back, okay?"

She beamed up at me, looking more girlish than she had since I noticed she was growing up on me. "Really?" She hugged me, squashing Sass between us while he squeaked a protest.

Hand in hand, we wandered for a little while, smiling and waving at eager merchants who beckoned us closer, clearly seeing our clothing and noting us for nobility of some kind though I hoped we'd both dressed down enough we wouldn't be recognized.

"My love!" I spun, startled as someone grasped my hand. I gazed up into a pair of amber eyes, glowing with amusement, and a handsome demon face reminding me of Quaid.

"Excuse me?" I found myself smiling in spite of myself as Meira giggled and Sassy growled softly, tail thrashing against her arm.

The strange young demon bent and kissed my hand, hot breath heating my skin. His eyes never left mine, a wicked gleam in his gaze as he gently drew me closer.

"My love," he breathed. "I've been waiting for you my entire life."

I had to laugh. Just had to. And yet there was a catch to my laughter and I found myself flushing with a mix of embarrassment and attraction. When I tried to pull my hand free, he clung to it, pressing it against his broad chest, my fingers touching his bare skin where his tunic lay open at his throat.

"I beg you," he said in a voice vibrating with emotion, "don't leave me ever again."

Okay, this was getting to be a little much. "Listen," I said, "it's all fun and games until someone loses a hand." I raised one eyebrow and nodded at his grip on my person.

He grinned back and released me, but slowly, the tips of his fingers lingering on mine. "Here," he said, turning and lifting what looked like a necklace from a table behind him. He draped it around my neck before I could protest. "Perfect for you." Again with the wide grin.

Cheeky. Very cheeky. But he was delicious and my demon was having a good time. If only he wasn't trying to sell me something…

Before I could offer a pert reply, he paled, retrieving the necklace in a snatch before bowing his head to me.

"Careful," he whispered before spinning and vanishing behind his booth and the heavy curtain hiding the back of it from the outside world.

That was… weird. I turned to Meira and Sassafras to ask them what was up when I noticed for the first time we were alone.

Completely and utterly. Alone.

Shoppers, vendors, you name it. All vanished.

That couldn't be good.

Syd—Sassy's voice reached me just as I felt a buildup of magic very close to me, with only enough time to wrap my arms around Meira and pull the three of us to the ground.

Something exploded over my head, blowing out the side of a stall and sending those hiding inside it scrambling, screaming. I rolled over, looking in the direction of the attack, my power flooding me as my temper snapped everything into focus.

A dozen masked attackers raced toward us, hands full of fire.

This was no challenge.

They were trying to kill us.

This at least I was familiar with. Roaring in fury, I leapt to my feet and charged, magic flooding around me, a mix of witch, Sidhe and demon followed by the flickering white of the vampire as Meira's blue family power lashed out in tune with mine. Shaylee reached for the earth and, though it was foreign to her, it still responded, rippling under the feet of the charging demons. Half of them fell, stumbling and crashing into each other even as the combined power of Meira and my witch magic sought the moisture in the air and the pressure of the wind, driving the two together with such force sharp shards of ice tore through their masks and clothing.

Most of them fled. Only two remained, a man and a woman from the way they carried themselves. The male whipped an arm back, amber fire ready to take me out only to fall back with a cry as the white power of the vampire struck like the end of a jagged whip, sucking his magic from him.

With that, they ran after their counterparts, threads of Meira's blue power nipping at their heels. I almost went after them.

Was about to in fact, when I was suddenly surrounded by guards, flooding the market while the customers and vendors emerged, talking loud and fast and pointing at me.

"Finally," I growled at one of them. "Weren't you supposed to stay behind and guide us back to the Seat?"

I had no idea if these were Dad's guards, but I took a stab at it.

Not his. Or at least, not here to protect me.

"Sydlynhamitra," one of them said in a deep, wooden voice, giant hand going around my upper arm, "and Hathenemeira, you are both under arrest for the illegal use of foreign magic."

22

I couldn't make out Sassy's words, but the meaning was obvious. I knew swearing when I heard it in any language.

Part of me wanted to join him rather than sit and simmer with my arms crossed over my chest and my face set in a mask of absolute fury. After all, I already knew why he was so angry.

We'd been set up. And not in a subtle way, either. Not even close. The attempt to make Meira and I use our foreign magic, illegal on Demonicon, was so blatant if I did start swearing it would be accompanied by some fireballs and the odd explosion for good measure.

Meira fumed beside me, and I could only imagine the look on her face mirrored mine. I refused to look at the massive guards surrounding us, to acknowledge them in any way. I was not giving them even a moment of my attention after they clearly abandoned us to be ambushed, only to show up at the most convenient time for our arrest.

"I thought demons were good at this sort of politics,"

I finally snapped at Sassafras when he ceased swearing to hum his unhappiness, ears flat to the sides where he perched on the arm of my chair. The floating transport moved more slowly than the parade vehicle had, and from the stares and whispers and pointing fingers I could only guess that was the point.

"Most are," Sassy snarled. "Obviously, whoever is behind this didn't think we were worth the bother of a more elaborate attempt."

Okay, was he actually pissed the attack wasn't well executed? Seriously? Though I had to admit, the more I thought about it, the more I agreed with him. It wasn't like we were actually in any danger. It was clear both Meira and I were more than a match for those who wanted us dead. I suppose I should have been nervous, afraid. Instead, all I could feel was fury.

How dare they?

"That's the last time they underestimate the Hayle sisters." Meira actually grinned, eyes tight as she fist-bumped me. I laughed out loud, making one of the guards twitch. Were they afraid of us?

Wicked.

"Regardless of your skills or arrogance," Sassy said, tone heavy with sarcasm, "the plotting against you has risen to the next level already. Not that I'm really surprised, but honestly." His snort was so loud I had to giggle, my anger fading to annoyance and humor. "Has my name fallen so out of memory they would try something this pathetic and expect it to reap results?"

"Well, it did in a way," I said. "They succeeded in making us use our alternative magicks."

Meira nodded, a little glum, her own rage disappearing.

"True," she said. "What's the punishment for it, Sassy?"

He paused. "Death," he said, though casually, as though tossing off a comment with little weight. "I'm not worried about that. I'm more concerned with escalation from here."

Um, what?

"Death?" I reached out and took Meira's hand, fierce protectiveness surging adrenaline through my body, her magic linking to mine. "They can try."

"Your grandmother will never allow it," Sassy said. "You're not some common demons. Besides, I have no doubt she has intentions for the two of you that require you breathing."

Nice to know. And I believed him.

"Could she have been behind this?" The transport came to a halt at the foot of the mountain, the elevator platform descending to meet us, a very agitated and anxious Pagomaris hovering at its edge.

"Doubtful." Sassafras stepped up into my arms as I stood and strode forward, pushing my way through the guards, Meira at my side. They parted without a word, almost shrinking back from us. I ignored Pagomaris's distress as I mounted the elevator and spun, demon cat in my arms, chin up and shoulders back as the platform began to rise.

"Grandmother wouldn't do anything like this," Meira said.

It worried me Meira was so willing to jump to her defense, but Sassafras beat me to speaking up.

"While I'm not as inclined to believe Ahbi's intentions are pure," Sassy said, "I agree with Meira. As I said, she has plans for both of you. This has to be an outside attempt to discredit the pair of you and, most likely, your father."

"It couldn't be Grandmother," Meira repeated, somewhat smug. "She's way smarter than this."

That at least I could agree with.

I could tell Pagomaris wanted to talk as she stood there, hands wringing before her. It wasn't fair to leave her hanging, but I wasn't in the mood to deal with her simpering or the clear anxiety she wore on her face.

Instead, I held myself rigid beside her, treating her like a servant, though it made my stomach churn. I didn't want to be mean to her. She had her orders and her own status to protect. But after the way we'd been treated here, I wasn't in the mood to play nice just to save her feelings.

I spun and marched to the back of the platform, stepping off at the top level before it even came to a halt. It was obvious where the guard were taking us and I'd be damned if I'd let them drag me before the court of my very judging family when I could instead use the opportunity to show them all who was boss.

Of course, it depended on my grandmother's good will whether I'd succeed or not, but I was counting on her being on our side. Sassafras was right about one thing—Grandmother had her own agenda and her plans for us that had nothing to do with bringing us physical harm.

No word on the emotional damage, but that part I could handle.

I felt the guards hurrying, as though they were trying to pass me without making it look like they were running. Instead, from the gaping stares and slightly angry expression on Vandelarius's face, they succeeded in making themselves look like my procession, not my captors.

I came to an abrupt halt at the foot of the dais, glaring up at Grandmother who simply stared back, face completely blank.

"Grandmother," I said.

"Sydlynhamitra," she answered in her rumbling voice. "Welcome, as always, my child."

She might have been a conniving, political animal, but she knew when to have my back.

Vandelarius looked about fit to blow a brain vein. Instead of exploding, he gestured abruptly, a glowing row of amber letters appearing beside him.

"Ruler," he snapped, "these criminals have been brought before us to answer for breaking our laws."

She didn't say anything, didn't look at him, just continued to hold my gaze.

Vandelarius cleared his throat, the simmering of his anger reaching me as his power rippled out. How had he advanced to Second Seat when he could barely contain his magic? I broke my grandmother's hold over me and turned to the smaller throne, my disdain as clear as I could make it in both my eyes and my body language.

"My sister and I were attacked," I said, loud enough the whole court could hear, "and defended ourselves against those attackers."

Vandelarius's eyes narrowed as the floating writing

sparked with his anger. "You used foreign magic inside Ostrogotho," he said. "That crime is punishable by death."

Muttering, whispering. It was clear by the level of tension in the family they knew we wouldn't be dying any time soon, but it was also clear a shift in power was coming. I could feel them leaning in one direction or the other, their demon power flowing around me as they aligned with their favorite throne. It didn't take long for Vandelarius's lack of support to make itself known.

Not that he was willing to give up so easily. "It can't be denied they broke our laws."

"After our guards conveniently abandoned us," I countered. Power twitched behind me. Did the gathered guards just flinch? Not that I cared, but it would have been nice to witness. I turned my attention back to Grandmother whose expression hadn't changed.

An angry voice grew louder, one I knew well, though I didn't turn to acknowledge Dad as he stormed his way up the procession to stand at my side. He quivered in fury, magic crackling around him.

"What is the meaning of this?" He focused his full attention on his mother. "My daughters were the victims here."

"Your daughters are law breakers," Vandelarius hissed, but it sounded more spiteful than powerful.

I didn't need Dad to defend me and when Grandmother's amber eyes met mine again, I knew she understood that. "Laws or no laws, I tell you this—if challenged according to demon tradition, I will fight with demon magic. But if my sister and I are attacked again with intent to do us harm, I will not hesitate to use every form of magic at my disposal to assure our safety."

"You admit to not only using your foreign power, but to the intention of doing so again?" Vandelarius's false shock revolted me as he swept the court with his gaze. "And we are expected to simply allow these two to wander our city, free and dangerous?"

"I warned you when we arrived," I said. "I'm not just a demon, but much, much more. And I have the right to defend myself and my family if our lives are in danger."

Vandelarius opened his big, ugly mouth to speak, but Grandmother's hand lifted and dropped down onto the arm of her throne, the sound of two boulders slamming together. He shrank back, sullen anger bubbling, while Grandmother spoke.

"Enough," she said, and that was it. The tension in the family faded, magic realigning and retreating. Even Dad settled beside me, though I couldn't bring myself to relax.

Grandmother waved the same hand she'd almost started an earthquake with. "Bring the boy here."

This time I did turn, out of surprise, to see the merchant boy I'd met slinking forward, two guards escorting him. He fell to his knees, face pressed to the stone floor as he shook so hard I worried he might fly apart.

"Rise, child," Grandmother said in a voice as kind as I'd ever heard from her, "and tell me what you know."

He looked up briefly, face a mask of terror. But when he spoke, his voice was at least level enough I could make him out.

"The ladies and their furred companion were attacked," he said. "I feared for their lives. But they defeated the dozen masked ones who ran away with their cowardly tails tucked between their legs."

Even obviously scared to death he had a silver tongue.

A tiny smile pulled at Grandmother's lips, but it vanished so fast I wasn't sure anyone else saw it. "I see. And did you witness the two using magic?"

"Yes, great and honorable Ruler," he said.

"What color was their power?" The intensity of her gaze was so fierce I suddenly wondered what she was really after.

"Amber," he said as the family gasped and Vandelarius

sat forward to protest, "wound through with blue, white and green."

"But the dominant magic?" She was as still as a statue, a predator waiting to pounce. "What color?"

"Amber, without a doubt, most powerful and benevolent Majesty," he said.

Grandmother nodded once. "You may go, with the thanks of your Ruler."

He scrambled backward on his hands and knees, somehow managing to bow as he did. He met my eyes a moment, his glittering in mischief, and I understood then the game my grandmother played. Who was he really? No common merchant. Was she having us watched? I returned my attention to Grandmother, mind churning, but pretty sure I now knew what she'd say.

"While the daughters of Haralthazar indeed engaged foreign magic," she said, "their demon power contained it." No one spoke up to argue with her even though I knew myself she was bending the truth. My demon chuffed happily, content to allow her to continue. "And considering this wasn't some simple challenge, but an attempt on their lives, it is my decision to pardon them of all charges."

I bowed my head to her, Meira doing the same beside me even as Sassafras began to purr.

"It is the order of Ruler you refrain from using your foreign magicks further, however." Grandmother was pushing her luck.

"As long as no one else tries to kill us," I said, "I'll do just that."

Okay, maybe I was the one pushing. But no way was I backing down on the issue. Vandelarius looked like he'd been forced to swallow something painful, so there was that victory. And as long as Grandmother didn't decide to hit me with a bolt of lightning, this day might not turn out so bad after all.

Her tiny nod was all the answer I received, but it was enough. I found myself breathing again, felt the entire room inhale and knew everyone had held their breath, held time even, waiting to see what she would say.

Grandmother rose to her feet. "Court will dismiss," she said. The family left without question, moving away in clumps and groups of more whispering. Vandelarius harrumphed his way from his throne and stalked off, a group of what had to be flunkies gathered around him, one female demon staring at us like we were dirt. Had to be Dad's sister, Vandelarius's wife.

So nice getting to know the family.

I was about to turn and leave myself when someone's

hand touched my arm. I glance sideways, found Pagomaris smiling at me. All of her anxiety was gone, at least the visible parts.

"Her Royal Majesty would like you to join her."

I glanced up at Grandmother, found her stepping down from the throne. Since she'd just saved our asses, who was I to say no?

23

Meira didn't hesitate, rushing forward to hug our grandmother. Yup, hug her. I found myself gaping as I fell in step beside Dad while the tall and imposing Ruler hugged my sister back.

I kept going to the place of wondering if she wasn't such a monster after all. Either that or she was just really good at manipulation.

I was betting on the latter.

Grandmother smiled at me as I stopped a few feet away, Dad at my side, Sassafras still in my arms. It seemed like a real smile, one setting her eyes alight with sparkling good humor.

"I believe a tour is in order," she said. "Allow me to show you our world as it was meant to be seen."

I followed, still a bit hesitant. But Dad didn't seem overly upset, though he frowned to himself, staring at the ground as we walked. And Sassafras was still purring, if softly, almost absently. Meira chattered away about the battle and her part in it as she walked ahead of us, the tall and imposing demon Ruler bending to meet the gaze of her much more diminutive granddaughter. It almost made me jealous.

Almost.

My heart pounded a few beats as we neared the edge of the room. This time there was no platform in sight, just a hole gaping out over the city. I glanced sideways at the rows of guards who stood at attention, lining the entry. I didn't exactly trust them anymore, not after they'd clearly betrayed Meira and me, not to mention Dad. And Grandmother. Still, she seemed relaxed and if I knew anything about her yet, it was the fact Ahbi Sanghamitra would never, ever trust anyone with her own safety.

We could agree on that, too. Was it weird I wished I didn't have so much in common with her?

Mouth dry from the view, I was grateful when a canoe-like platform zoomed up and came to a halt at the precipice. If a canoe was the size of a stretch limousine made for giants. Grandmother swept her way on board, taking a seat as it formed in the center. A smaller one gelled for Meira. When I stepped behind Grandmother, assuming Dad and I would be relegated to the back, she gestured for me to join them. And wouldn't you know, two more seats appeared, facing her.

All we needed was some jingle bells, snow and horses and we'd be sleigh riding. How quaint.

Sassafras chose to curl up in my lap, ignoring the protruding bed my chair provided for his comfort. I watched with curiosity as it retracted into my seat again and wondered at the magic controlling the vehicle. Was it Grandmother who ran the show or was the thing itself somehow working its own wonders?

I didn't get a chance to ask. Pagomaris bowed as the sides of the car rose, thinning out as they did, forming a clear dome over us. I opened my mouth to ask what the deal was only to have my stomach lurch upward into my throat as the whole thing dropped like a stone.

My stomach lodged firmly in my throat was all that kept me from screaming we were going to die. So I was grateful, really. I had just managed to shove my intestines back into their proper places, drawing a deep breath to express my concern with our imminent deaths, when I saw Meira laughing. Heard her, too.

Only then did I realize we weren't falling any longer, but cruising at a very fast pace, the bubble of our transport whipping through the air so quickly the land beneath us flew by.

Grandmother smiled at me again, though I was sure this time the humor was aimed at me rather than with me. "We have far to go if you are to see everything," she said. "I thought this would be the best option."

"We could ride the veil." Yes, I was being snarky. Feeling very put out to be totally honest. Didn't doubt even for one second Grandmother knew about my fear of heights and decided to let me suffer a little for challenging her.

"We could." She bowed her head to me just a little. "But I thought the ride would be nice. A chance to speak freely with only our family to hear."

Did that mean she didn't consider the rest of the brood to be family?

How interesting.

"I'm unsure how much your father told you about your home." Yeah, jabbing at Dad now. He looked away, refusing to meet my eyes, gaze locked on the scenery though his hands clenched in his lap. There were times I almost liked my grandmother. Few and far between. Now wasn't one of them. "Or what history has been shared."

"A little," Meira said. "About the planes coming together. The four cities."

Grandmother nodded, patted my sister's hand. "Indeed," she said. "Many millennia ago, a handful of brilliant scientists brought the planes together, under the leadership of your great-great-great grandfather."

Meira beamed at her, soaking it up. So the Zel Sass mentioned was an ancestor. I glanced sideways at Dad and found him frowning still. And Sassafras was uncharacteristically silent, which made me wonder.

"What was once fractured and broken," Grandmother said, gesturing out the glass bubble, "is now whole, beautiful. Complete."

I peered out, finding it easier to look down from my seated position, my vertigo not affecting me the same as when I stood. And the view beneath us, rapidly approaching as the vehicle dove, distracted me so much I hardly felt the drop.

We swooped rapidly toward a gushing waterfall, the froth as pink as Kool-Aid. I stared, mouth open, billowing clouds of mist engulfing us, plunging us into pale rose shadow.

"What was wasted is now combined with purpose." Grandmother's voice droned on as we cut through the water suddenly, and into open air. I looked up as moisture sheeted cleanly from the bubble, not a drop left behind, grinning at the roller coaster feeling as we rose again rapidly, climbing the seemingly endless cliff of the waterfall, more massive than anything we had at home. "What was reviled is now embraced and accepted." I heard Dad grunt softly, Sassafras's snort, but I was so wrapped up in the scenery as we flew past a flock of what I swear were horse-sized dragons with the most amazing multi-hued bodies and reptilian wings, I let their reactions go. Not like I was paying attention to what Grandmother said, giving it any credence. After all, she was selling us with the skill of a time-share master.

As we rose to the surface again, amazing water left behind, the chasm a black line fading behind us, flock of mythical beasts spiraling into the mist, I didn't really care. She could try to sell me all she wanted as long as the tour went on.

Freaking cool.

I met Meira's eyes and found her grinning too. The pair of us must have looked like total morons, but I didn't mind that either.

Spike-like spires rose on the horizon as Grandmother went on.

"What was once war now is sport, to increase our power and the stability of our people."

The city grew before us, totally different than Ostrogotho. Where the Seat city was dominated by blocky buildings resembling the mountain, this place soared, appearing as dangerous as it was beautiful, shining peaks of sharpened metal forming the pinnacles of each roof until the whole getup reminded me of a very elaborate pincushion.

"Our differences once divided us. Now we work together for common goals. And common good."

The craft soared around the city, circling closely enough I could see etchings in each spire, the entire place looking like it was crafted by an artisan jeweler. It was beautiful but frightening to look at, and I couldn't get past the impression the demons below lived inside a deadly weapon.

Our vehicle turned, heading into the multiple suns lighting the sky. The bubble tinted softly, enough I didn't have to squint as I looked down over the vast greenery below. Had to be a rainforest, thick and dark, a winding river running through the impossibly solid canopy.

"And so things have been for many generations." Grandmother's voice was that of a tour guide, cajoling and calming. "Demonicon has been at peace because of the system we have developed and the joining together of all demon planes."

Dad tensed beside me. I felt it, the change in the air between us. A glance toward him gave me nothing aside from the same scowl he'd been sporting all along, but I knew then Grandmother wasn't being totally honest.

Surprise, surprise.

Still, if that was the case, what was she hiding. And why?

Anger showed up, my demon answering with her

own. "Thanks for the company line," I snapped without thinking.

Grandmother's eyes met mine. Any moment I expected to be pitched over the side and sent screaming to the trees below, now thinning, no longer the type that might catch me and save me from so high a fall. But she didn't react, just gazed over her world. It was Meira's look of anger that really gave me pause as she reached out and took Grandmother's hand.

"It's beautiful," Meira said.

"Yes," Grandmother said. "It is, now. But only with strong leadership will it remain so."

Another city appeared, this one more rounded, domes glistening in the multi-suns. It was almost rainbow like, casting reflections toward us. Large domes and small, some as tall as the waterfall we'd seen, others almost tiny, clustered together to form a large metropolis, though smaller than the last.

"Is that what's worrying you?" Meira looked up at Grandmother, her own face pinched with anxiety. "That Demonicon doesn't have strong leadership?"

The old demon stroked Meira's hair so kindly I felt another jab of jealousy even while I told myself to stop being such an idiot for falling for her little game. "It does,"

Grandmother said as she met my eyes. "But not as strong as I'd like."

"And whose fault is that, Mother?" I almost jumped when Dad spoke up. He'd been so quiet, so withdrawn since we came on board I never expected him to say anything. His eyes flashed anger, though sullen and cold.

"Mine, of course," she said without a moment of hesitation. "For not insisting certain things come to pass."

They stared at each other a long moment, Dad glaring and Grandmother expressionless. I almost laughed out loud, considering how similar their relationship was to Mom and me.

Of course their little spat had much bigger consequences.

"No matter," Grandmother said as we spun away from the domed city and headed out across what looked like a desert, the ground red and glistening in the light. "Things have changed in the past and shall change again. It is the nature of life."

I stared down at a massive herd of elephant-like creatures, head spinning. I really had nothing else to compare them to. Though I was well aware our elephants weren't the size of houses with black skin shining like jewels or long, stumped tails they used as a fifth foot.

Meira practically leaned into Grandmother's lap to see

them, spinning and turning in her seat as they vanished. This time I did cry out as the floor beneath us went transparent, the herd, thousands in number, galloping away in the distance as we flew on.

"Our family has ruled on Demonicon since it was formed," Grandmother said as the floor retinted and my heart started beating again. "I intend for our dynasty to continue."

I met her eyes as she stared at me again. "There's a risk otherwise?"

"If Vandelarius gains First Seat," she said, "then yes. His line will take over."

Interesting. "You have lots of kids, don't you?" I felt Sassy tense in my lap and wondered if I was pushing things too far. "Make one of them Second."

Grandmother laughed, low and rumbling. Even Dad smiled at me, a weak one, but a smile.

"It's not that easy, Syd," he said.

I sat back, trying to keep my curious gaze from studying the next city we'd come upon, the perfect lines and angular shapes of the irregular buildings begging me to study them. This was more important, clearly. No way was I letting Grandmother distract me from so serious a conversation.

"I've seen you in action," I said to her. "Don't tell me

Vandelarius is Second when you didn't want him there, because there's no way I'll believe it."

Grandmother bowed her head to me, just a little. "You've raised a very talented and intelligent daughter, Haralthazar."

"Two of them," Dad said.

Grandmother smiled down at Meira and nodded. "Two of them."

The car lurched suddenly, forcing me to grasp Sassafras with one hand and the chair with the other to stay in my seat.

"Ruler," a voice that sounded like Pagomaris filled the car, anxious and tight. "You must return immediately."

Grandmother straightened, her normal flat expression returning. "What's happened?"

"Nothing." Her hasty denial was enough to make me tense. "Only that Nunaresh requires your immediate attention."

That wasn't the name of one of the cities, at least not that I could recall. Who then was Nuneresh? I looked out over Grandmother's shoulder as the car jerked again, just spotting the peaks of what looked like another city in the distance. Weren't there only four?

And, um, was that smoke?

"We're on our way." The car zipped even faster, the

landscape below whipping by so fast I had to look down at Sassafras so I didn't throw up. He met my gaze, his own flickering with fire.

Yup, something was definitely not right.

"Mind telling us what's up?" I caught sight of the mountain rushing toward us even as Grandmother's amber eyes flickered to mine.

"Were you interested in being part of this family," she said, "I might consider it."

Oh no, she did *not*.

I jerked in my chair as the car lurched to a sudden halt at the platform. We'd toured most of the plane in what seemed like minutes, though I was well aware the distance we'd covered would have taken us hours, if not longer, by airplane.

Grandmother left us, gesturing for Dad to follow. He scowled at her, but did as she asked, pausing one moment as Meira and I left the car.

"Go to your quarters," he said. "I'll meet you there."

"Dad," I said. "What's going on?"

"What's always going on," he said, voice bitter. "Just go."

When would he learn not to boss me around?

24

We were almost back to our rooms, Sassafras still in my arms, his weight actually becoming a burden, when Pagomaris appeared with two guards beside her. She looked uncomfortable, as though she was about to do something she really didn't want to, but her smile smoothed out as we approached.

"I hope you had a wonderful tour," she said, tone bright as ever.

"Would be better if we knew why it was cut short," I said. No need to be careful what I said to her, at least.

Pagomaris hesitated, her smile faltering before it returned full beam. "You've been summoned," she said to me. Meira took a step closer, but the tall demon aide smiled sadly down at her. "Just Sydlynhamitra."

I wasn't expecting Grandmother to call on me at all, let alone without my sister. Not after the snarky family comment she made. But the look on Meira's face was even more unexpected. She actually seemed furious with me as she spun and stomped her way into her room, slamming the heavy door behind her.

Sassafras squirmed enough I let him down. "I'll take care of it," he sighed, silver tail quivering as he went after her, power easing the door open just enough he could slide through before letting it fall closed again.

I scowled at Pagomaris as I spun to go to Grandmother's room. "If her plan is to turn my sister against me, she's got another thing coming."

Pagomaris grabbed my arm as the two guards stepped in front of me, blocking my way. When I met her eyes, there was fear in hers.

"This way, Princess," she said, a soft tremor in her voice.

Okay then.

"What's this all about?" I tried to catch her gaze again, but Pagomaris kept hers locked on the floor ahead.

"I surely wouldn't know," she said, glancing over her shoulder.

The guards. Nice to know they really couldn't be trusted. But that also meant because of them I wasn't getting the information I needed, and that made me testy. They followed so close I felt them breathing down the back of my neck. Testy times a million.

They didn't want me testy times a million.

I finally stopped dead and turned to glare at them. And while I didn't say anything, exactly, I did let my demon out for a moment, really out. She tended to be pretty scary, even for a demon.

Needless to say, the big boys backed off.

"Dish," I hissed at Pagomaris as we approached a doorway. On my right was a full wall of nothing but city in the distance, the left solid stone. I kept to the inside, grateful for the demon aide beside me blocking the view. But as she spoke to me, my eyes couldn't help by wander over the world far below.

"Be cautious," she whispered so softly I barely made her out. "Not your grandmother."

That was all the warning I had before the door in front of me swung open and I was led inside.

While Grandmother's quarters were opulent and dark, they now seemed reserved compared to the garish and overly bright space I found myself in. Not quite as big as Ruler's, just close enough I knew it had to drive Vandelarius crazy. His clear lack of taste was reflected in the clashing colors and bling bling everywhere. I suddenly wished for the tinted glass of the car dome as Pagomaris bowed low and presented me to Vandelarius.

He squatted on a large chair—might I say throne?—

perched on a pedestal in the center of his chambers. He obviously thought the whole getup intimidating. Or maybe it reinforced his need for a sense of importance. Either way, I just thought he was pathetic. I'm sure it showed on my face, because his tightened, eyes flashing fury as he gestured with anger at the guards behind me.

"Your Highness," Pagomaris said at her most bright, "Her Highness, Princess Sydlynhamitra, as requested."

I hope he wasn't waiting for me to bow, because we would both be in for a really, really long wait if that was the case. Or maybe he just thought glaring at me was getting him somewhere.

Whatever.

"I'm here," I said. "What do you want?"

Pagomaris hissed ever so softly next to me, but no way was I taking crap from this guy if I wouldn't take it from my grandmother. Not when I knew he wasn't nearly as powerful as me.

Seemed I was more demon than I'd first thought. All of a sudden, power was everything. And I knew, could see it in how his body hunched, how his nasty little eyes narrowed, he understood just what I thought of him.

"I hope you and that bratling sister of yours are happy," he snapped.

"Not really," I snapped back. "We have to put up with the likes of you, don't we?"

Again the hiss from Pagomaris, this one more obvious.

Vandelarius leaned forward, power pushing out before him. "I'm sure Ruler hasn't informed you in some foolish attempt to protect you, but I have no such worries for your wellbeing." I felt certain he didn't care about anyone but himself, so that wasn't much of a shocker.

Though what he came out with next absolutely was. "Because of you and the threat you both present, one of our cities is in civil war."

Um, what?

"Nuneresh." I made the connection, glancing sideways at Pagomaris who nodded just a little. Holy. Civil war—over us? Why?

Vandelarius sat back, smirking now. "That's right. And if the pair of you remain much longer, revolution is likely to spread to other cities."

"And why exactly is that our fault?" No way was this pudgy demon playing princeling going to blame civil unrest on me or my sister.

"Because," he snapped, "they've been calling for fresh rule, for a new family to lead them. And with you two here, with your father's advancement, the people now know your grandmother never intends to release her hold on Demonicon."

Why then did Grandmother insist on the opposite, that our family needed to hold on tight, that Demonicon needed us? She'd made no mention the rest of the populace wanted new blood to lead them. Well, if they wanted another family, it made sense she'd be fighting tooth and nail. But there was no way the pus bag sitting on his fake throne before me was a better alternative.

"Hear me, daughter of Haralthazar," he said, "the throne is mine and belongs to my line from now on. When the old bitch dies, my family will be in control, my son Second seat." What little I'd seen of Cypherion didn't make me feel any better. "And nothing will stand in our way."

"Okay," I said, going for casual. "Knock yourself out. I don't want your stupid throne anyway. I'm going home—remember?"

"Deceitful child," he snarled. "I know better."

Call me a liar, will he? "Listen," I said, "let's get something straight. You're the one all hot and bothered over the succession. Maybe you have a reason to be worried. Maybe you don't. But if I catch you threatening my family again, law or no law, you'll see what real magic can turn you into."

It struck me then, with his beady eyes glaring at me,

exactly who had set us up. He was just enough of a moron it had to be his plan.

"And if you want to kill me," I snarled, taking a step toward his little throne while the guards rustled in concern behind me, "do it face to face, you coward."

"How dare you address your Second Seat in such a manner!" He surged to his feet, pointing at me with one disgusting finger. "Guards, seize her and have her charged with threatening her ruler!"

I felt them moving, shoved them back very firmly with my power, a sense of recklessness taking me over. "You want to give it a go, Vandelarius?" I let him feel my demon as she stretched and pulsed with power. "Feel like challenging me?"

He glared, face crumpling, and I knew he considered it even as my brain screamed at me I had lost my freaking mind.

"Your Highness." Pagomaris broke our moment, stepping forward, bowing at the waist, smiling, hand on my arm, pulling me back. "There has been some misunderstanding. Her Highness understands completely the weight of her position, the strength of yours." Her fingers tightened in warning. "Completely."

Vandelarius sagged back in his seat, eyes still smoldering, but I was sure he was happy she'd given him an out.

Total douche bag.

I turned and left without another word, shaking in anger, wanting more than ever to just go home and get the hell away from these people and their insane way of life. I knew I'd end up on a short fuse for weeks after spending so much time on the edge of my rage, but it was the only thing that seemed to keep me going so I embraced it.

Pagomaris hustled along beside me, the two guards no longer following at least. We were almost to my door when she reached out for me again, pulling me to a halt. She smiled widely, too widely, fake and strained.

"I will see you soon, Highness," she said. And hugged me.

I almost pushed her away, especially when her power surged around us both.

Listen carefully, she sent in the tightest beam I'd ever felt. *He will kill you if he can. And your sister. Your father. Do not challenge him unless you are ready. He appears weak, cowardly, but he is Second Seat for a reason.*

She let me go, still smiling. "Be well, Princess."

Pagomaris left me there, stewing, but with food for thought, to turn and go inside alone.

Sassafras waited for me, Meira beside him, perched on the bed. My sister looked chagrined as the demon cat spoke.

"Wasn't Ahbi, was it?"

I sighed heavily, throwing myself down beside him. "Stupid Vandelarius," I snarled. "Jerkwad."

"You can say that again." Meira slid over to me, snuggling against me. "I'm sorry," she said. "I was really jealous."

"Tell you what," I told her, "next time you can go. Okay?"

She giggled. "No thanks. You can have him."

I sat up, pulling her along, Sassafras squashed between us. "It was Vandelarius who tried to kill us," I said."

Sassy nodded. "I figured it had to be," he said. "He's the only one who could command the guards to abandon you."

Meira pulled up her legs and hugged her knees. "What did he say?"

I filled her in on the civil war while Sassy hissed.

"It's not your fault," he said. "At least, not the way he told you. Your grandmother's speeches about unity and all of demon kind coming together aren't quite accurate. There has always been unrest. Discord. Those who would see the planes broken apart again, or at least given their own rulership, something they lost when the present system came into play."

"Poor Grandmother," Meira said. "It must be really hard to rule this whole place."

I didn't agree with Meira's emotion, but her sentiment was accurate.

"There's a reason she has such a useless ass as her Second," I said, reality dawning.

Sassy sighed. "I have to agree," he said. "It's likely Ahbi assisted his rise to ensure no one would support him if he chose to challenge her."

So freaking sneaky. I might not have liked her much, but my respect for my grandmother went up several notches.

"So she advances the worst possible choice so the people would have no choice?" I threw up my hands, pacing again. "I thought she wanted Dad beside her."

"She's pushed him, yes," Sassafras said, "but considering the incredible power your grandmother wields, I've always wondered why she's never forced your father to take his place. Now it's beginning to make sense."

"She wasn't ready." Meira nodded, a firm, sharp motion. "But now she is."

"She's sown the seeds of his rise," Sassy said, "but it wasn't until now, for whatever reason, her timetable is imminent."

"We're sure it's not Syd?" Meira met my eyes, worry in hers.

I shuddered. No way in hell could anyone convince me to take over this place. Then again, there'd be some changes. Even better. Or worse.

Sassy's tail flicked as he considered. "I have no idea,"

he finally said. "Ahbi is a mystery even to me. But you can be certain whatever her plan, Vandelarius is not part of it."

"And if she's underestimated him?" I stopped my pacing. "Is that possible?"

Again Sassy paused. "I wouldn't put anything past any one of your family," he said.

Just lovely.

I so had to get out of here.

My demon spurred me up. "Let's go wander," I said. "I can't stand speculating and the air in here is killing me."

Meira's answering grin probably shouldn't have made me smile. Especially knowing what we were purposely walking into. Not that I was looking for a fight, mind you, but I had a big wad of pent-up anger energy burning a hole in my gut and I couldn't stand to have it there another minute.

Four battles for me and three for Meira later and I was feeling much better. And stronger, which probably helped a lot. Sassafras's continued sharp discontent with my fighting ability did nothing to quench my satisfaction. I won. That's all I cared about.

After dinner with Dad, quiet and uncommunicative despite my pointed questions, I'd had enough. Sassafras left with him, supposedly to get answers, though I knew the demon cat knew more than he was telling. Unwilling to be a pawn any longer, I proposed a plan to Meira, one she immediately accepted. That night, rather than waiting for Pagomaris to retrieve us one at a time, my sister and I went together to visit our grandmother.

The guards at the door looked startled to see us, but when I knocked the doors swung wide easily, welcoming the two of us before closing on the unhappy guards.

25

"Welcome." She stood near the sofa as usual, dressed in her silken robe, arms open to Meira who rushed forward to hug her. I took a seat before such a welcome could be offered, though I thought a hug for me would be a long time coming. Meira perched next to Grandmother, helping herself to the snacks spread out on the low coffee table.

"You're aware Vandelarius is trying to usurp you?" Yeah, she knew already. All of our speculation was dead on from the small, smug grin she suppressed. I resisted the urge to roll my eyes, falling into grumpy.

Grandmother didn't seem to mind the lack of small talk. In fact, her amusement grew into a full-grown smile at my pronouncement, sitting back with one arm over the back of the sofa, Meira sliding back to snuggle beside her.

"Of course," she said. "He spoke to you earlier."

Not a question. "Told me the civil war going on in one of the cities is our fault."

Grandmother snorted, still amused. "I'd hardly call it

civil war," she said. "There has been some unrest, yes. But not over the two of you."

Meira looked up at her. "Then why, Grandmother?"

"I'm afraid it's my fault again," she said. "I've been Ruler too long, the longest of any Ruler in Demonicon's history. My own father stepped down centuries before his time. But I'm not prepared to hand over control of the assembled planes to just any demon. And certainly not to someone like Vandelarius."

"Then why did you make him Second Seat?" My anger rose again and forced me to my feet, to pace in front of the vast hearth. "So no one would want you to step aside?"

It was a big accusation, and I wasn't sure she'd appreciate me calling her a manipulative bitch, or at least implying it. Instead she stroked my sister's hair like she owned her. "I'm certain you know to keep your friends close," she said in answer, "and your enemies closer."

"Mom tried that once," I said. "With a witch who betrayed us all." Even now, almost a year later, my rage at Celeste Oberman and her attempts to undermine and overthrow Mom still burned strong. Especially knowing not booting her sorry ass meant the deaths of witches I loved.

"And how did it turn out?" Grandmother seemed genuinely interested.

"Not so well," I said. "We lost some very good people because she wouldn't act." Okay, not exactly fair. I had the chance to rid us of Celeste too but let her stay, thinking the way Mom did. Keeping Celeste near meant keeping an eye on her.

Yeah, not so smart.

"You have to trust me," Grandmother said, "that I have many more years of experience at this than your mother does."

Fair enough. Still.

"You also need to do the same," she said. "Though the more I get to know the two of you, the prouder I become."

That was a shocker.

"Thank you, Grandmother," Meira beamed.

"I am thousands of years old," the demon Ruler said. "I've birthed hundreds of children, all from different mates, searching for the perfect progeny." She sighed, looking suddenly tired and old. It was strange to see her vulnerable for even a second, and of course it didn't last. "None have been up to my standards, nor the standards my own father set for me. Conniving, petty, small minded, all of them. Until your father was born and I knew, I knew he was exactly who I'd been waiting for."

The idea she'd discarded her own children in the search

for the perfect ruler made my skin crawl. Still, I'd met some of her kids, at least been under their judging eyes, fought their children and I had to agree with her they weren't the nicest bunch.

"I worried your human blood would ruin you," she said as my anger rose again. "But I am pleased so far. You are both worthy of my bloodline."

Even Meira looked uncomfortable while my fury let loose.

"You don't own us," I snarled. "We're not creations, we're people. And we choose what we do and for whom."

I'd seen her blank and cold. I'd seen her tired and old. And I'd even seen my grandmother smile as though she meant it. But until she rose from that sofa, her power surging around her, amber eyes full of fire, I'd never seen her angry.

Oh boy.

"You must learn," she said, voice booming thunder, magic crackling around her in a storm ready to strike me dead, "if you are to take over my Seat."

So Sassy was right. She wanted me to rule.

"Thanks," I said, refusing to back off despite the fact I could feel how much more powerful she was, that the briefest touch from her magic in that moment could have crushed me like a bug, "but no thanks. I already have a job."

She pushed. Hard. And I pushed back. Held my ground. Barely.

Oh, just barely.

"I need you, Sydlynhamitra," she said, voice softening as her power ebbed. "Your world needs you. Your father."

"No," I said. "My coven needs me more."

She stilled a moment, shrugged at last, her power retreating. "Perhaps," she said. "But what about a century from now? Two? Will you not grow bored of leading lesser beings as time goes on?" Her amber eyes burned me up as I processed what she said. "What will you do then, my child?"

Um. Whoa. What?

"What?" My brain swirled, contracted, fought. No. Freaking. Way.

"I assume then your father, in his stubbornness, didn't tell you everything." Grandmother shook her head. "He is a fool, and yet, these very traits are those that have produced so much power in the two of you." She fixed me with her blank Ruler stare. "During the experimentation, when Theridialis attempted to find a way to return Haralthazar to Demonicon, he uncovered the truth about you, my dear.

The fact you are as long lived as I am. As your demon cat. And as your father."

I heard Meira gasp, but couldn't look away from the huge demon before me. "You're lying."

Grandmother smiled. "I'm not," she said. "And though I know you don't trust me, or believe me, it is the truth. You are far more demon than human, Sydlynhamitra, despite your appearance on the other plane."

And just what did she know of me on the other plane? Where was she getting her information?

"What about me?" Meira's little voice squeaked the question while my heart clenched and all of my thoughts liquefied, running out of my head in a fearful rush.

Grandmother's smile turned sad. "You will live a very long life if you remain here," she said. "As long as any demon, because of your blood. But if you choose to live on any other plane, your human side will dominate. How odd, the two of you—one who appears a demon, but is human, and the other her opposite." Grandmother reached down and touched Meira's cheek. "If you decide to return to what you call your home, you will grow old and die like any human."

Tears trickled down Meira's cheeks, and I found she wavered before me as my throat tightened, a hand of ice crushing my soul as my mind aged my sister in a spinning whirlwind, turning her into Gram with horns and faded red skin.

"No," I whispered. "It's not fair."

"Fair." Grandmother's voice was full of bitterness. "If only there were such a thing, my child." She straightened and faced me again. "I am willing to wait for you to grow bored of your little coven," she said, "if that's what it takes. But you must learn to survive here if you are to rule in my place someday."

Her bitterness was catching. "Well, I'm trapped here, aren't I?" I turned from her, arms over my chest, but resisting the urge to hug myself. I would not show further weakness.

"You are," Grandmother said. "Which means you'd better get used to the idea."

Round three.

Ding, ding. Damn.

26

I left shortly after, unwilling to talk to my grandmother any longer, dragging my sister out with me. She allowed us both to go, though I felt her eyes boring holes in my back as I retreated, head spinning with new knowledge and the fear I really was trapped here forever.

Meira jerked free of me the moment we were out of sight of the guards. I turned to her, not meaning to be angry, and certainly not mad at her, but my anxiety had the best of me.

"We have to go see Dad." Man, was I going to ream him a new one.

She glared at me, rubbing at her arm where I'd held her. "Says who?"

This was no time for back talk. In fact, the expression on her face reminded me of the brat she'd been after returning from a summer at witch camp, turned to the dark side by the evil of the Dumont family. No way was she regressing to petulant child on me, not with so much at stake.

"Meems," I said, "what the hell?"

"Don't tell me what to do." She turned away from me, face set in a pout.

If she said I wasn't her mother, I was going to scream.

"Fine," I snapped. "I'm going to see Dad. You stand here and act like a child."

I turned my back on her, frustration driving me to take a step away, though I had no intention of really leaving her behind, when a ball of demon power struck me between the shoulder blades, staggering me.

It wasn't a very big ball. And thanks to my training I had lots of shields built up anyway. But still.

She was so dead.

I turned, rage flaring, to see Meira sobbing silently, face in her hands. Okay, crappy big sister moment, obviously. I rushed forward and hugged her while she struggled to be released, though she didn't fight me too hard and ended up hugging me back after only a moment.

"Meems," I said. "I'm sorry. What's wrong? What did I do?"

She shook her head, face pressed into my shoulder. "I love Mom and Gram and everyone," she whispered. "But I love it here, too." She looked up, eyes wide. "Even the fighting." Like she was saying something bad. "I feel whole for the first time in my life." She sagged against me. "I'm a terrible person."

I rested my cheek on the top of her head and sighed. "No, you're not," I said. "You're allowed to be happy, you know that, right? On your own terms?" I shoved aside the image of her so aged and tried to just be there for her without my own fears spilling over and making things worse.

"It's just... you get everything." Meira backed away, face contorted as she struggled with what she was feeling. "I don't mean to be jealous of you, Syd," she said, more tears flowing down her cheeks, "I really don't. But I can't help it sometimes."

Jealous? Of me?

"You're the coven leader," she said, shoulders sagging. "You have two guys in love with you, both amazing." Okay, kinda true. But way off base, if she knew how I struggled with them. "You're beautiful and don't have to hide it." Sigh. "And now you get to live forever and be Ruler and everything." She threw her hands up in the air. "And I get to stay home and die. That's just great." She stared at me with her heart in her eyes. "Can't I just have one thing?"

I'd done everything I could, or thought I had, to make sure Meira knew how important she was to me, how much I loved her. I always thought I'd done a good job, was a good big sister. But obviously there were things I'd missed, perceptions she had I couldn't begin to fathom.

"Meems," I said, opening my arms as she rushed to me again and held on. "I never, ever want you to feel like you're second best."

"I am," she said, almost a wail.

"No way," I shot back. "No. Way. You are amazing and beautiful and unique. No one is like you and never will be. I love you so much, you know that. And I only ever want for you what makes you happy."

She snuffled. "Even if that means I want to stay?"

"Absolutely," I said, heart breaking. What would I tell Mom?

Oh, right. Trapped. Problem solved.

"I love fitting in here," Meira said as she pulled away, wiping at her cheeks with both hands. A little smile emerged. "No one stares for the wrong reasons and those demons I fought, they were scared of me after." She went a little pale. "That's bad too, isn't it?"

"Not here," I said. "You want them to be afraid. And they should be. You kick ass."

She giggled. "I do." Her amber eyes glittered with almost evil glee as she shed the last of her upset. "So do you."

"Not according to Mr. Bossy Pants." Meira giggled again at the nickname for our demon cat.

"I'm a really good fighter," she said, "and I know I'd

do well here. Make it to Second Plane someday, I'm sure of it."

"You should be there now," I said.

Meira hesitated before blurting, "Grandmother offered me an advance in status to match yours if I stayed."

The bitch. As much as I understood my grandmother's political motivations, it pissed me off to no end she manipulated my sister and her need to feel like she belonged—and now to keep herself from a human lifespan—in order to get what she wanted.

"She said I'd have a place at her side, be royalty. Second to no one." Meira blushed. "But that's not true, is it? The only way I could be first is if I was Ruler."

My stomach clenched. "I'm sure she was just trying to help."

Meira nodded slowly, face falling. "She's been playing me, hasn't she?"

"She's really good at it," I said.

My sister had always been sheltered, acted younger than her age for a long time, loved and coddled by the coven. But the last few years had undone most of that. The mature young woman who met my eyes, despite her mere ten years, made me feel old.

"Let's go talk to Dad," she said.

As we headed for the platform and Dad's quarters below, I knew we had to find a way to get home even more now. Before my sister took her new knowledge out on someone.

I reached for Dad as we stepped onto the platform.

Coming your way, I shot at him, not pulling my anger.

What's happened? He reached for me, but I shoved him aside.

You have some explaining to do, I sent. *No more secrets.*

He pulled away and severed the connection, but not before I felt the sadness in his mind.

So it was true, then. He already knew what I was going to confront him about.

Wonderful.

When the elevator slammed to a halt, I was so wrapped up in my thoughts I almost didn't catch myself, falling to one knee instead of flat on my face. Meira cried out, keeping her feet, but swaying like she'd been struck.

Fear grasped me by the throat and shook me as my mind went immediately to falling. Something was very wrong and all I could think of was plunging, the useless platform underneath us, the mile or so straight down to the street below.

The sight of four masked figures landing in our midst drove the fear out and let my anger take over. I welcomed it, surging to my feet, my demon emerging full throttle, roaring in rage, leaping for the first one who slid sideways and went over the side with a cry.

No shields. The fear fought my fury, trying to crawl out my throat and scream itself to death, but I couldn't fall apart, not with my sister fighting a masked assailant, two more coming toward me.

I drew in my power, calling on all of my magic, Shaylee and the vampire coming to my call just as the two entered my personal space. Vines of magic snaked out, taking first the female, then the male around the ankles, jerking their feet out from under them, sending them sprawling. In that moment I knew who they were, but the information did me no good as the girl, recovering first, dove for me while her partner shot at me with a bolt of amber fire.

It was easy to block his attack, but I was too slow to avoid her completely. She tackled me, pulling me down, rolling over on top of me, so close to the edge I could barely breathe. I heard Meira scream my name just as the male side of their little team pounced, the girl sliding away, his feet impacting my hip and sending me spinning over the edge of the platform and into open air.

My fingers caught the lip, just barely, power of earth burrowing deep into the stone as Shaylee caught and held me with her energy. Panting, terror slowing everything down like a horror movie, I couldn't scream because I couldn't breathe.

I had to pull myself up. Use magic. Do something. I felt my demon energy roar, the pooling of my witch power, reaching, pulling, shoving me back up.

Only to have my link to the platform severed as the wards came back on.

I had one final glimpse of my sister reaching for me, screaming my name, before I fell.

27

There was an odd excitement to falling I hadn't expected once the initial terror burned off. The air rushed past me in a gale, whistling in my ears, though the passion of its passing tore at my clothing and forced my body to ripple uncontrollably. It took me a few seconds to get past the idea of dying before my demon roared and shook me, taking control of our magic, diving for the veil.

Only to meet the same stone wall as before, even the rubbery membrane out of reach.

This time she wasn't taking no for an answer and neither was I, damn it. Forget this dying shtick—not while I had power to fight it. I reached deep, pulling from all of my magicks, leaning into the veil as hard as I could. Shaylee and my vampire core poured energy into my demon, now more powerful than she'd ever been.

And in that moment, while my body slowly spun sideways, as I now faced the ground rushing toward me, what was once tiny and antlike now alarmingly large and growing bigger by the second, I felt the veil soften, weaken.

And part.

We were inside in a flash, about a breath before the ground made me into something gooey, the slickness sucking me along in the dark, welcoming me home. My demon roared again, in delight this time, even as my body quivered in reaction to our near death.

Meira. I didn't have time to think of myself. I let my anger have its head, surging through the edge of the veil to the platform, slicing through the wards and landing next to my sister as the three assailants tried to pull her off the elevator and down a dark tunnel low on the mountain.

She'd done well, her power blazing around her, but I wasn't about to let her fight alone.

One of them ran at the sight of me, disappearing inside, but the other two took one look and flickered into the veil.

Oh *hell* no. I grabbed Meira and tore the edge open, flying after them. It was different inside this time, trying to track them. But I could feel them still, the echo of their passing, though by the time I figured out what I was doing they were long gone. Their persons, anyway.

They left their fear behind for my demon to snarl at in satisfaction.

I dropped us out in Dad's quarters, Meira grinning up at me with a fierceness triggering my own toothy snarl, though she shook as much as I did now that we were safe.

"Thought you were dead," she said, punching my arm as Dad leaped to his feet at our sudden arrival, Sassafras staring, Theridialis also half out of his chair, gaping like a suffocating fish.

"You too," I said, punching her back. I met Dad's eyes, letting him see how much anger I still had inside me. "That was a rush."

"Do tell," Sassy said.

Boy, did I. And when I became too furious to speak, Meira took over. I spent the rest of her tale in my typical pacing back and forth, hands clasped behind my back so tightly I didn't think they'd ever come apart.

Dad sagged back in his chair as Meira wrapped up, staring at me like he didn't know me.

"Syd," he whispered. "Are you all right?"

"I was tossed over the side of a mountain," I said. "What do you think?"

"And yet," Theridialis said, eyes narrowed as he stood and came to my side, power tickling along the edges of mine, "you managed to use the veil. Despite the fact it was somehow closed to you. Interesting."

"Does this mean I can go home now?" Home. Yup. Please and thanks.

"I don't think so," he said. "But there is hope now, yes?"

Hope. Lovely.

I spun on Dad, able to talk again. "So about this whole living forever thing?" I jabbed a finger into Theridialis's round belly since he was close enough to vent my rage on. "When were the pair of you going to get around to telling me?"

Dad had the good grace to look tragic. That's how I was feeling, kind of, so it diffused a little of my anger. "It's not just because you're half demon," he said. "While we are exceptionally long-lived, you, my daughter, are truly immortal."

Theridialis was nodding. "Consider, you also carry the soul of a Sidhe princess inside you, my dear. An immortal spirit tied to yours."

"And now you have the vampire essence as well," Sassy said. "Immortal number two. Add your demon's extended lifespan and it's not exactly a shocker, Syd."

All of my rage vanished in a sudden need to feel sorry for myself. I crossed to the table and sank into a chair, sadness taking me over. This sucked, big time. It meant I'd outlive everyone I loved.

Well, not everyone, maybe. Sassafras came to me and climbed into my lap, putting his paws on my shoulders, head-butting me with his fuzzy forehead.

"I've said goodbye to so many Hayle witches," he whispered. "It'll be nice to have you around for a while."

I hugged him, tears brimming. Now I knew how he felt, or could imagine it. Bad enough to have to see Gram die someday. Mom. But people who I was supposed to grow old with?

Oh. My. Swearword.

Quaid.

Liam.

Love.

I couldn't do it to either of them.

Sassy pulled away, met my eyes. "Don't go there," he said, as though knowing what I was thinking. "Besides, the way you fight you might not make it to nineteen."

Smartass cat.

Just what I needed.

"Maybe Grandmother is right then," I said. "Maybe I should stay and forget going home. At least here I'm not the only one."

"Syd—" Dad started.

I didn't let him finish. "Come on, Dad, think about it.

I'm already in enough trouble with the coven and the Council for being part demon and all the other stuff I carry around with me. You know I make them nervous." Mom did her best to hide it from me, but ever since I took the vampire essence inside me she looked at me a different way. I guess she had the right.

Then again… "Unless Mom knows already?"

Dad shook his head, all the answer I needed.

"Now that I know I'm immortal, do you think the coven will be okay with that? Or the other powers that be? Not likely." I stroked Sassy's fur. "Staying on Demonicon makes the most sense." I met my sister's sad eyes. "And for Meira, too."

But as I sat there, surrounded by glum demons, I wondered to myself how I could go through with it. How could I just abandon my family without telling them what I was, giving them the chance to ask me to step aside?

And thoughts of the two guys in my life didn't make things any easier. Quaid at least was mostly out of the picture despite the fact I wished things were different. But now I knew I could never be with Liam. He wasn't immortal and the thought of falling in love with him then losing him was just too much for my heart.

So much for love, then. How much did my life suck?

28

I woke the next morning in a foul mood. As I stood in my closet, looking at the hideous clothing Pagomaris stocked for me, the full-length mirror throwing back the image of a very pissed off demon girl, I made a decision.

I dressed aggressively in spiked boots and a pair of skin-tight pants in some kind of black leather with studs all over them. The shirt was also tight, a heavy jacket with matching spikes and a few skulls with horns decorating the shoulders and cuffs finishing my attire while a collar jutted out an array of spines I had to be careful of so I didn't stab myself by accident.

My hair I bundled up in a mess of angry curls, tied off with a chain and several blades. When I checked out the mirror again, I smiled. Yeah, badass.

Time to take out the trash.

Meira's eyes went wide when she saw me before she grinned like the devil she was at heart and ran for her own wardrobe. By the time I'd finished breakfast, Sassafras glaring at me from his place on the table, thick silver tail thudding up and down as his ears sat flat, Meria emerged from her room dressed like me.

"They want a piece of the Hayle sisters?" She snapped her fingers, cocking one hip to the side, feet planted wide like some pint-sized action heroine. "Big mistake."

I laughed. And agreed with her.

No more Miss Nice Syd.

I went hunting, my sister at my side, angry demon cat trailing us, hissing and spitting his upset. Not like I cared. That morning alone I started and finished a dozen fights, Meira cutting her own swath through the ruling elite of Demonicon's Seat until the lower status ran from us like rabbits.

Sassafras finally decided to help after he got over his snit, filling us in mentally on the different cousins we called out, letting us know their weaknesses and flaws. So we wouldn't get ourselves killed, he said. But with each fight, despite his former concern, I sensed a growing, if grudging, admiration for us, and by the time he was fully behind our campaign of doom, there was real enthusiasm behind his notes.

She fights with her left side only, favors her right.

His shields are strong from the outside but he never reinforces the inside.

He favors bashing. Use finesse.

She can't get past her own cleverness. Just whack her.

After a nice lunch where Meira and I grinned at each other like loons, partly because we couldn't believe we were actually still on a roll, we continued our task, swelling with power and driving the cousins before us like cattle.

Couldn't fight, huh?

By the time the main sun was setting, I felt able to take on Grandmother herself, demon power crackling inside me. It was getting harder and harder to find anyone to fight, so we'd descended into the city, searching for prey. I refused to fight anyone who wasn't family and Meira followed my lead. A few had fled into the lower planes and were easy enough to track down and defeat.

I found myself, at last, standing over one of my *dear* cousins, a girl with a scar on one cheek, her red skin white in a line down the side of her face. She'd been an easy defeat, almost crying when I cornered her and drove her to her knees, muffling her power with mine. She cowered there, begging me not to hurt her, offering up her magic as my demon hummed her satisfaction. It was odd at that moment, to notice Shaylee and my vampire were missing, the sense of disgust they'd left behind as they walled themselves off making me feel a little nauseated. Still, this was what I had to do if I was going to be a demon, live in their society.

I reached for the girl's power and felt it—the entirety of it. She was offering it all to me, not just the selection I'd grown accustomed to. The deliciousness of her fear and the surging magic she held out to me was so tempting, I reached for it.

Syd! Sassy's mind cut across mine like a whip. *No!*

I pulled back, feeling my demon grumble and retreat, now fully sick to my stomach. I waved the girl away, turned from her, finding myself in a back alley in some part of the city I didn't even remember reaching, squat buildings crouched around me, streets empty and very quiet as though the local populace knew exactly what was going on and refused to bear witness. My target scrammed, but not before I caught the relief and gratitude in her eyes even as I sank back against the stone wall of one of the buildings and caught my breath.

"Syd." Sassy came to me, Meira with him, paws on my leg. "You need to stop."

I nodded, bending to pick him up, the anger gone, my demon rumbling her contentment even as Shaylee and my vampire emerged and settled into their places.

"I almost did what you did," I said, the sick feeling subsiding slowly. "I almost took her power."

He hesitated before nodding. "There's someone you need to meet."

Sassy hopped down and led us out into the street, a few brave souls risking a venture out, only to scramble for safety when they saw us. The sight made me feel even worse, like I had become the monster my grandmother wanted me to be. I kept my head down as we crossed two streets and ended up at a ground level train station. This time I didn't worry about being alone, despite the fact this station was much plainer, without the gilt and creative decoration of the higher levels. Somehow the serviceability felt homey, more relaxed, though I didn't for a moment let my guard down. At least the few passengers waiting for the train didn't seem to care who we were, just as happy to mind their own business, though I figured the way I was dressed wasn't helping my reputation on the lower planes any.

I shrugged out of my jacket, stuffing it into a waste receptacle, hearing the hiss of magic as it was destroyed. The spiked collar went with it, though I salvaged the blades from my hair, sliding them into my boots just as the train hummed to a halt, wards dropping to allow us to enter. Not that I'd need a knife or anything, but I wasn't taking any chances.

As I stood, the shields snapping into place as the

train began to move, my body swaying slightly, I found myself scowling. The veil was right there, the edge of it as welcoming as it had always been. We could just ride it again, instead of being good little demons, but I held my peace. When I really needed access to the veil, if we were attacked, for instance, it was comforting to know I could take my sister and Sassafras and leave.

Maybe. After I kicked the bad guys' asses and cleaned the floor with them.

Okay, so not all of my aggressiveness was gone just yet. But I could live with that.

The train ride was longer than I expected. We'd ended up somewhere in the Fourth Plane region, but Sassafras had somewhere much more remote in mind. He refused to answer any of my questions, sitting alone on one of the chairs, huddled in a silver ball. I finally gave up and looked out the window, lost in thought.

The ride gave me time to think about the veil and my sister. Despite her attempts at home, and mine to teach her, Meira had never been able to access it, to ride it the way I did. Neither of us could figure out why. Dad didn't seem to have a problem, nor Grandmother. Maybe it had to do with Meira's being more human than demon.

Another thing for her to resent me for.

Glum, I disembarked at the last station behind Sassy and my sister, where the shadow of the mountain barely reached us, two suns still up though the sky was darkening, several moons chasing them. The streets here were clean, but plain, the buildings less ornate. But there was still a sense of nobility about it and I wondered where Sass was taking us.

He paused at the door of a small house, neat and tidy, a pert little garden out front, before going to the door and using his power to ring the bell. It chimed softly from somewhere inside and, before I could ask him any more questions, the door flew open and a pretty young female demon smiled at us.

When she looked down and her eyes focused on Sassafras, they flew open very wide. With a cry, she bent to her knees, bowing to him.

"My lord," she said. "Please, be welcome."

Sassy looked uncomfortable, tail flickering side to side, ears flat sideways, whiskers low.

"Mistress Sophelara," he said. "We're here to see him."

She stood at once, bowing again. "Of course. Please, come inside."

Bemused, exchanging a curious look with Meira, I followed Sassafras into the house. A demon man stood waiting, his eyes as wide as the woman's as he bowed too.

"Lord Sassafras," he said. "We are honored you've chosen to come to our home."

Why did my demon cat look so unhappy with such a nice welcome? The nicest we'd had since we arrived. I was actually feeling pretty comfortable in their lovely little house, but his reaction immediately squashed my ease.

"Knight Deerinalon," Sassy said. "How has he been?"

"The same, my Lord," Deerinalon said, gesturing for us to follow down the hall and to the last door on the right. "How kind of you to visit. This way."

The moment we entered the small room, I knew, understood. And my heart broke.

Sassafras padded his slow way forward through a cluster of toys, across the cluttered floor, to the side of the young demon who played with two wooden blocks by smashing them together with terrible timing. With the grin of a small child, he dropped both and reached for my demon cat.

"Momma!" His voice shrieked, almost tearing my eardrums. "You got me a kitty!" He focused on Sass, a thin line of drool running from the corner of his slack mouth as he grinned at my demon cat. "Kitty," the boy said quite seriously, "would you like to play with me?"

Sassafras sat down, tail covering his front paws as if he needed it to defend himself from the disabled demon before him.

"Hello, Raneen," Sassy said. "You don't remember me."

I glanced sideways at his parents, saw them gazing at Sass with adoration. I expected fury. After all, this had to be the boy Sassy stripped of power, the cause of his banishment. From the crippled look of him, the child-like way he lived, Sassy's attack had left their son permanently damaged.

Why weren't they furious?

"Lord Sassafras is so kind," Sophelara said to me as she caught me staring. "He made certain our Raneen was taken care of. He even had us raised in status." She smiled in wonder. "I used to be 138th Plane. Now we're twenty-fifth. If it weren't for Lord Sassafras, we would never have advanced so high, nor had the ability to care for Raneen."

I gaped at her in shock while her husband slid his arm around her shoulders.

"We'll never want for anything again," Deerinalon said. "And neither will Raneen."

Raneen reached for Sassafras, pulled him into his lap. My friend lay limp, allowing the boy to stroke his fur, sing a silly song to him about kitties and soft fur. But it wasn't long before Sassafras sat up and bolted, running between my feet and down the hall toward the door.

I went after him, murmuring thanks to the couple, Meira already ahead of me.

"Is his Lordship displeased with us?" Sophelara looked so afraid I stopped and took her hand.

"Not at all," I said, watching relief come over her face. "We just need to go. Thank you for having us."

She and her husband waved goodbye as I chased Meira and Sassafras.

I didn't have far to go. My sister crouched in a nearby alley, stroking his fur while he turned his back to her, body shaking. I bent and scooped him into my arms, cuddling him against me. Sassafras twisted to the side, paws around my neck as he cried on my shoulder.

Meira's hands pressed to his back as I gently held him until he was done.

Sassafras finally pulled away, his fur wet, eyes flat and lifeless.

"Now you know," he whispered. "Both of you. Please, be careful."

We both immediately agreed and I knew, no matter how far I was pushed, I'd never go so far again.

I guess I should have expected it. But sadness clung to all three of us, slowing our steps, making us inattentive. Not like it mattered, really, but I would have liked to have known my life was in danger.

Normal state of affairs, so it served me right.

Twenty or so masked attackers appeared on the train, our car conveniently emptying of riders as the last of the suns went down and night took the city, bathed in the soft pink glow of many moons. I rose to my feet from the molded seat, so not in the mood to deal with these jackasses, not even a flicker of fear crossing my mind, unable as well, oddly, to muster my anger. Instead I faced them with irritation and annoyance, power crackling around me as I beckoned them closer.

"What are you waiting for?" The two lead masks didn't seem hesitant, but their pack of followers weren't so secure. I felt them wavering just from the focus of my attention, their magic quivering, made worse when Meira rose to stand beside me.

"Aw, what's the matter?" Meira winked while two balls of demon fire formed around her hands, bouncing like toys ready to be thrown. "Scaredy cats?"

Sassafras snorted.

I lashed out, my magic jerking the masks free, Cypherion and Tanasharia glaring at me now their identities were exposed.

Oh so obvious, cousins.

"Sad, right?" I spoke to Sassafras in my most bored tone. "A little originality would have been appreciated."

"Not from these two," he said, the King of Haughty, either recovered from his visit or hiding it in his best Sassafras fashion. "You're simply expecting too much."

"We warned you we were going to take care of you two," Tanasharia said, but she was all bluster and hot air, her power no match for mine.

"Cowards," I snapped. "You want to fight? Come fight. Otherwise, get lost."

I didn't wait to see what they'd choose. I was done waiting.

My power hit them both in the guts, bending them in half, leaving it to Meira to clean up the rest of the attackers, now a terrified mob running from our car to the next to escape her flashing balls of fire.

I'm not sure what they were thinking, or if they were prepared for how strong Meira and I now were, but before either of the cousins could escape or fight back, I had them wrapped up in so much magic it was a wonder they didn't suffocate.

Easy, Syd. Down, girl.

I turned to Meira with a grin. "Nice job," I said. "Proud of you."

"You too." She eyed the cousins critically. "Think his could be a little tighter, maybe?"

She was right. Cypherion was inching his way free, already reaching for the veil. Despite his higher status, I was surprised to feel his magic was weaker, less solid than what I had control over. The fact I was now stronger than the heir to the Second Seat wasn't lost on me as I snapped the shield tight again, hearing him moan with some satisfaction.

Okay, with a huge, honkin' dose of *hell yeah*. Happy?

"I think it's time to take this little party on the road." Sassafras thrashed his tail. "I'm sure your grandmother will be delighted to discover what her family has been up to."

I loved my demon cat. So. Much.

I was a good sister. I let Meira have Tanasharia. She did a great job, too, constant prodding of the shields holding the pair her idea. I'm certain it was pretty uncomfortable, at least from the moans and groans coming from the unhappy siblings, but it was a great way to test and be sure we didn't have any weak spots.

Sure it was.

The train ride was uneventful the rest of the way, our elevator trip to the top of the mountain equally as quiet. Calm before the all-out crap storm. It was almost a relief to emerge in the throne room and face the music, dragging our charges behind us with ropes of power, Sassafras perched on Cypherion's head as though he were the conquering hero.

As far as I was concerned, he was welcome to the title.

I had no idea Grandmother was holding court, though the fact was pretty obvious the moment we set foot on the top of the mountain. No way was I backing down now, not with the whole family watching.

Quivering.

Um. Well. Wicked.

Vandelarius leaped to his feet long before we reached the thrones, spluttering and even redder in the face as we stormed our way down the concourse and finally dumped the two cousins on the shiny stone before Grandmother. If they grunted from the impact, I wasn't sorry. Sassy hopped down with great aplomb and stood at attention, silver fur shimmering with amber fire.

Dad struggled at the edge of the crowd, a handful of guards holding him back as his rage burned them, but he stilled when he saw we were all right. Grandmother herself had paused when we appeared, floating golden paperwork fading as she watched our approach. Now she sat as she always did, face a stone mask, eyes empty and cold as I bowed my head to her just a little.

"Grandmother," I said.

"Sydlynhamitra," she said. "I take it this situation has an explanation?"

"It does," Meira said.

"Release my children at once." Sounded like Vandelarius had a hold of himself at last. Grandmother's eyes flickered to the side, the barest frown of irritation tugging at her lips before she focused on us again.

"Explain," she said.

I began to, with the attack the night before, how it was the same masked people as the first time, when Vandelarius interrupted.

"You rode the veil?" He spun on Grandmother as everyone gasped softly, whispers breaking out. I was so tired of their whispering. "Will you continue to allow your progeny to destroy our laws? No one is permitted to ride the veil in Ostrogotho."

"They you'd better lock up your kids," Meria snapped. "How do you think they reached us?"

Grandmother nodded.

"Go on," she said, while the entire court held its breath.

I threw the two masks to the ground. "They tried to kill us three times," I said. "First, in the market." I tapped into my witch magic, the hell with the rules, and cast the image of the event up, over our heads. All eyes turned toward it, murmurs of excitement rippling through the family. Even Grandmother looked up, though her expression never changed. The scene unfolded from my point of view, intermingled with Meira's as she added to the show, the family magic more than happy to produce the hologram in our defense. "Then on the elevator, as Meira said." This time I let them fight with me, battle the cousins, slide over the side. Gasps of terror, a few shrieks, told me I was getting my point across. I let them fall with me. Touched them with a breath of air magic, allowed them to feel the rush of the wind and saved them, just in time. Plunging the vision into darkness as my memory entered the veil. "And just now on the train." It was hard to hold my demon back after I'd let her have her head all day, power built up and ready to use while the family magic finished the show, complete with the cousin's unmasking.

The image flickered and went out, the entire family exhaling and shifting, eyes now locked on me and my sister, many of those eyes full of wonder. For a race that lived on magic, I was surprised such a display gave them pause.

Not the display, Sassafras sent. *You're commitment to each other. They have no idea what real love is, remember?*

I'd had enough. Sickened and frustrated to the breaking point, I focused on Grandmother.

"I demand satisfaction."

That got the family going at last. Chatter erupted, no more whispering. Dad hovered nearby, glaring at Vandelarius. But when he tried to move forward, I latched onto his mind.

Not yet. I can handle it. I promise.

He didn't move. Though I could tell I had to hurry or he wouldn't be still much longer, guards or no guards.

Grandmother held up one hand and silence fell. Just like that.

"There is only one way to settle this," she said. "A battle to empty."

I thought they were quiet before. Shock makes a great silencer. I just wish I knew what she meant and why it was such a big deal.

Empty, Syd, Sassy sent. *Like Raneen.*

Oh crap.

Vandelarius looked back and forth between his kids and us, licking his lips like we were good to eat. "A battle to empty hasn't been invoked in centuries," he said, oily smooth. "But I agree, Ruler. Clearly this situation warrants such a contest."

He thinks they can beat you, Sassy sent. *What does he know that we don't?*

Dad broke free with a roar so loud it echoed back from the stone walls. Guards tumbled to the side and he was suddenly in front of me, body hunched, sparks flying from him as he shook with fury.

"Absolutely not," he rumbled, facing down not only Grandmother, but his brother-in-law. "They attacked my daughters. They need to be punished."

"And they will be," Grandmother said. "In the battle. If your daughters are powerful enough for the task. Our ways demand it, Haralthazar."

There were enough nods of agreement I knew we weren't getting out of this. Dad's aggressive stance folded, shoulders going back, grim expression telling me he'd lost before he began.

So much for justice.

"You will only use your demon power." Grandmother's face grew suddenly harsh. "Any use of other magicks will be seen as cheating and will be punished with death."

Not that I needed access to my other powers, considering how much magic I'd stored up in my full day of ass whooping. But it still wasn't nice of her to cut our throats like that.

"These are serious charges," she said. "Only our most serious trials can end this dispute. We must trust in the system we have created, no matter our feelings. Our way is through battle. And in battle justice shall be found."

I didn't like how happy Vandelarius looked, nor his kids, as Grandmother's power severed our hold over them, Cypherion and Tanasharia suddenly free and glaring.

Not good, Sassy sent. *You're stronger, but they are more experienced. And without your alternate magicks to support you... this isn't the same fight you won on the train, Syd.*

Not much we can do about it now, right? I snapped at him, tension mounting. *A bit of positive reinforcement might work better.*

He sighed. *Just be careful.*

Was he serious? Not helpful.

"You will fight together," Grandmother said. "Two against two."

Now it was Vandelarius's turn to look worried.

Sneaky and all kinds of awesome. Sassy was suddenly giggling like a little kid. *I'm going to kiss Ahbi when this is over.*

Can you fill us in? Meira's mind was in mine, connecting the three of us.

She just did you the biggest favor ever, he sent. *Think about it.*

Um. A little on the brain fried side at the moment, Sass. I didn't mean to snap, but this was no time for a life lesson. Or guessing.

But Meira's mental gasp told me at least one of us wasn't as slow.

One on one we'd lose, she said, without a hint of shame. *But together...*

I met Grandmother's eyes, saw her nod just the barest bit toward me.

Before I could finish processing, she drew a breath, shields snapping into place around the four of us, Sassy scrambling out of the way just in time.

"Begin."

Okay then. Not much warning, was there? I dodged as Cypherion threw a ball of fire at me, just slamming more power into my shields in time to prevent it from setting me alight. Meira went the other way, already lashing at Tanasharia with long whips of flame.

Remember what I said before? Sassy was right there in my mind still, my demon humming and howling for me to let her out. *Forget all of it. Do whatever it takes to bring his ass down.*

Raneen's face flashed in my head. *I don't know if I can. I said I never would.*

Cypherion will kill you, Sass said bluntly. *And Tanasharia will kill Meira. Have it your way.*

My demon was more than happy to come out to play.

31

There's only one way to win this. Meira's mind latched onto mine. *We have to work together.*

Brilliant. Sassy was right. The moment I could, I'd make up for not hugging my grandmother. One look at the pair before us and I knew what she figured out long before I had—our love for each other was the biggest advantage Meira and I had.

What the entire demon population seemed to be missing.

I let my sister link to me without hesitation, feeling the odd sensation of her body moving in tune with mine for a moment. It was almost distracting enough to get me in trouble as I fumbled my magic in the instant of our connection. But thanks to that same connection, Meira was right there with me and able to pull up the slack, her power feeding mine, a combined one-two of fireballs and whipping flames saving me from the lashing magic Cypherion let loose.

Let's take them down. I had to grin at Meira's grim yet

excited tone, the classic clichés coming from her. Too many action movies, I guess.

She wasn't the only one.

Our combination began to pay off immediately as the pair of cousins stumbled over each other while Meira and I fought as one. Though the brother and sister team had clearly decided on which of us they wanted more, the fact both of us fought them together threw their divided attacks off easily. I found myself grinning, Meira laughing next to me. She'd been so right. If we'd been forced to fight them one at a time, it was likely neither of us would have survived. They just had too much combined experience. But that was their downfall, ultimately—the fact they couldn't work together.

Meira and I slashed and cut and bullied our way through their attacks and defenses, pushing them back against the edge of the wards protecting the two thrones and the rest of the family, finally crushing them between our power and the sizzling shields.

Well done. Sassy's mental voice reached us. *Very, very well done.*

Seems we'd impressed him finally. Wonders never ceasing and all that.

Seeing the cousins panting and terrified before us was all the encouragement I needed.

Time to finish it. Meira fist-bumped me before I turned to Cypherion and reached for his magic.

I'd grown used to taking a portion of magic each time I fought, so the feeling was familiar. And I'd been fully prepared, my demon in total control, to strip the scarred girl in the city below. But what I didn't count on was the pain I felt reflected back as I drew more and more power from my cousin. My feeling of triumph faded as he writhed in agony, still pinned to the shielding, eyes wide, hands opening and closing in claws of desperation.

I started to ease off, unable to complete the draining even as my demon screamed for more.

You must. Sassy's mind prodded me sharply, desperately. *You have to finish him or all of this has been for nothing.*

I can't. I pulled away even more, the drain turning to a trickle. *This isn't right.*

Maybe not, Sassafras sent, *but it's necessary. Look at Vandelarius.*

I let my eyes rise, focused on the face of Cypherion's father, saw the evil hope in him as he realized I couldn't go through with it.

He doesn't care about his son, Sassy sent. *Only the fact if you fail he will win. Do you understand? Your life is in your hands—and your sister's. Your father's. Mine.*

My stomach knotted tight, heart pounding painfully in my chest as I met Grandmother's gaze. She hadn't changed expression, still as blank and cold as ever.

I don't want to be her. It was desperate, that message, sent to my faithful friend. His love wrapped me up and held me tight.

You never will be, Sassafras sent. *You are far more than she could ever hope to be, Sydlynn Thaddea Hayle. But you know there are times when a leader has to do what's best for all, not just for her. Finish what you started.*

He was right. I knew without a doubt he was. But it didn't help any.

Perhaps I was wrong about you. Grandmother's mind cut through mine like a blade of disappointment. *You aren't worthy after all.*

My fury lashed back, cutting her as deeply. *You have no idea.*

Teeth gritted, back straight, I turned up the heat on Cypherion and did my duty. But not for her, never for her. For my real family. As my cousin crumpled, his pain searing me as the last of his magic surged into my body, my demon near hysteria from the power of his agony, I told myself I would never, ever take my grandmother's place on the throne.

Ever.

But I did at least understand why draining other demons was no longer permitted outside of special circumstances. It was as though my demon was suddenly high on pain, boiling away inside me, begging me to turn on Tanasharia, the need for more power fed by the pain she'd caused. No wonder it was forbidden and why demons had such a bad reputation. If this was a normal reaction, it was amazing my ancestor was able to convince them to stop stripping each other empty.

Lucky for me I wasn't just a demon. With Shaylee and my vampire core to help, we wrestled her under control. When I finally felt like I was back in command I looked up, panting, to see Cypherion crumpled to the ground, shivering and vacant, amber eyes dull.

Vandelarius was on his feet, shouting something while the family made their own noises, an echoing cacophony I could barely hear through my demon's begging to be set free. I turned slowly to Meira who stared at me with fear in her eyes, but her determination was more powerful.

She must, Sassy sent, his sadness as crystal clear as the truth he spoke. *When it's done, you have to control her.*

I reached for my sister. *It's awful,* I sent. *But you can handle it. I'll be right here.*

She nodded once and turned to Tanasharia. The demon girl quivered in terror, twisting and turning, trying to tear free of us, but I grimly held her in place while Meira's power jerked hers free.

"Wait! Stop!" Tanasharia's desperate cry made Meira pause. "This was all Father's doing!"

Now silence again. Vandelarius's face twisted in rage, his power lashing at the shields between him and his daughter, but couldn't break through.

"Lying little traitor!" He rose to his full height, magic blazing around him.

"It's true, Ruler, believe me." Tanasharia wept, crumbling under the weight of our energy. "It was his idea to kill the newcomers, to discredit Haralthazar, to ensure they could not interfere when he had you assassinated."

Oh boy. The smile spreading across Grandmother's face had nothing to do with humor.

"Go on, my child," she rumbled as guards pressed forward to surround Vandelarius. His power no longer crackled, but sputtered, his face paling, belly jiggling as he began to shake.

"Ruler," he said, "you can't believe a word from her lying mouth."

Grandmother's hand came down on the arm of her

throne, power coiling around him, pulling him down into his own seat. "I will hear her out," she said in her booming voice, "and you will be silent."

Tanasharia, eyes alight with the chance she might be spared, spilled her guts. Everything from exact times and dates of conspiracy meetings to who was with her when we were attacked to the type of poison Vandelarius had just procured and the chef he'd bought to begin slowly killing my grandmother.

I watched Ruler carefully as the girl spoke, absolutely certain not a word she spoke was news to Grandmother and appalled by the fact she'd allowed the plan to go as far as it had.

When Tanasharia rattled to a stop, her trembling was worse, whole body twitching in our power. I finally let her go, leaving her for Meira to take, but my sister retreated as well, disgust on her face.

The wards protecting the family from our battle fell as Grandmother glared at Vandelarius. Her rage was obvious, power spreading outward, the family cringing, some fleeing in terror though most remained, sick fascination on their faces as though unable and unwilling to leave such a fascinating show, while Dad stood rigid and furious. No fear there.

"You have betrayed your throne," Grandmother said, rising to her feet, body stretching and growing until she towered over all of us, a giantess, a titan, amber eyes like beams of pure sunlight, her voice making the mountain tremble. "Vandelarius, I disown you." Amber power shattered in a rush of broken shards, the shining bits winking out like campfire sparks. Vandelarius cried out, falling forward, grasping his chest as the throne itself dumped him on his hands and knees. His power suddenly alone, unsupported by the Seat, pooled and eddied around him, uncertain, as though even his magic knew how much trouble he was in.

Grandmother ignored him, turning her gaze to me, huge hands gesturing. "Sydlynhamitra, it is time. Take his power and your place at my side as Second Seat and serve your people."

Holy.

It's not like I didn't expect some grand announcement from her, but no way was I expecting this. At least, not now. Me? Second Seat? But—

We knew she was planning something, Sassy sent, mind like a whip, breaking me out of my gaping stare and stunned freeze. *I warned you she might try something like this. You have to turn her down.*

Easier said than done.

Still.

"I'm not next in line." As if I wished this on Dad. He stood there in silence, eyes locked on me, though he looked more sad now than angry.

"I call on you to challenge," Grandmother said. "If you are able to defeat Vandelarius, you claim Second Seat."

So much for that argument. Not much of one anyway. It was Dad or me. And neither of us wanted the job.

"No." It was the best I could muster, but from the scowl

on her face I knew my best wasn't good enough so I tried again. "I am a coven leader, daughter of another plane." That was better. Get a grip, Syd. "My duty lies elsewhere. I can't take the throne."

Grandmother's magic lashed around me, but didn't touch me, sending more of the family fleeing in fear of her. They were all afraid of her, all of them. Except Dad. And, as it turned out, while I stood there and felt her power push me around, me.

"I'm a free soul," I said, keeping my voice level though I wanted to show her she had no hold on me. "I choose, I decide. And I will not be bullied."

Grandmother roared, the shields holding back the outside world rippling, a breeze breaking through the vast bubbled dome surrounding the top of the mountain. She stomped one step toward me, hands reaching for me, but I blocked her with my power, Meira's fed into mine, joined by Sass and, with a surge of rage that shocked me, Dad.

She backed off then, but her anger was still as powerful, the air thick with it.

"You have run roughshod over our laws," Grandmother boomed, "but no longer. You must challenge Vandelarius and, if you defeat him, his Seat is yours. You have no choice."

Why me? I sent it quickly to Sass and Dad.

Cypherion was his heir, Dad sent back while Sassy hummed his unhappiness. *Because it was Vandelarius who ordered your death and you defeated his heir, you must now fight his father.*

And if I say no for real? I shuddered at the press of Grandmother's power, not from fear but the sheer energy of it. *I can't, can I?*

You'll be stripped, Sassy said sadly, *for disobeying the Ruler's order and your power given to Vandelarius. He will then remain as Second Seat.*

Well, that was freaking stupid. *Even though he wants to kill Grandmother?*

I didn't make the law. Sassy grunted like the truth hurt.

Dad, I sent, desperation clutching at my heart as the truth hit me. I couldn't stay here, couldn't be trapped on a throne. I had to go home, had to keep trying, no matter what it took. *There has to be another way.*

Dad's power hugged me close. *There is,* he sent. *And if I hadn't been so selfish for so many centuries, this would never have happened.* His amber eyes locked on mine, a sweet smile on his face. *But I will never regret any of it. I love you, Syd.*

Before I could stop him from doing what I knew he was doing, all the while feeling like he was somehow saying goodbye, Dad turned to his mother, power surging. He rose, body growing as hers had, like he'd done at Mom's trial, until he stood shoulder-to-shoulder with Grandmother, family scrambling from underfoot, Dad's power snapping and crackling around him in surges of amber lightning.

"This has gone far enough," Dad roared. "You've finally won, old woman. Are you happy?"

Grandmother stilled, the surge of her magic pulling tightly to her. "Declare your intentions, Haralthazar."

"You've orchestrated this whole mess," he threw his words at her with power behind them, ricocheting from her shielding, but she did nothing to stop him. Vandelarius skittered away from them, finally regaining his feet, staring up at Dad in absolute hate. "You've always wanted me in Second Seat. All the lies and deceit and trickery, really, Mother. Just to have me finally where you want me." Dad's voice eased back to a low rumble. "I've never wanted this. And yet, you refuse to leave me be. But as much as I can tolerate you manipulating me at every turn, I won't allow you to use my daughters any longer. Nor will I let you force my child into ruling beside you."

Grandmother simply stared at him. "Declare yourself," she repeated, a smile growing on her face, grim and self-righteous.

Dad turned to the fallen Second Ruler, drawing his power around him. "Vandelarius," my father cried in a voice that shook the mountain, "I challenge you!"

Just like the cold-hearted snake he was, Vandelarius was prepared, surging immediately into massive shape to confront Dad, lashing out with his power without warning. I spun toward Meira, our power forming a protective shield around us and the scrambling Sassafras, just avoiding the fallout of the attacking demon's power. We ran for cover, away from the main concourse, just as Dad's massive hands latched onto Vandelarius and tightened around his rival's throat.

Not just a battle of power. The two grappled with each other physically, Dad's fist impacting the smaller demon's face. Vandelarius spun sideways, energy pushing him up even further, making him bigger, shoulders pressing into the shielding around the throne room. Dad lunged forward, fists impacting the other's guts, but Vandelarius's magic lashed out at the same moment, leaving burning welts across Dad's chest, his tunic shredded and hanging from his muscular chest.

Dad roared, body swelling further, joining Vandelarius in a push against the sky while his magic flew from his clawed hands into arrow-shaped fireballs, puncturing Vanderlairus's shields. The Second Ruler flew backward, landing hard, sliding along the polished floor, taking out part of a wall with his massive fist while the shielding flickered and fought to keep the dome contained. Dad went after him, us following. I held Meira so tightly to me it felt as if we were one person, gasping in fear as Dad bent over Vandelarius to deliver a blow only to have him fly back himself, landing hard on his back over the two thrones with a groan of pain, a large, smoking circle in the center of his chest.

Dad! I reached for him, feeding him power, Meira and Sassafras doing the same. Dad surged to his feet, shaking off the attack, only to have Vandelarius shriek in fury.

"Not allowed!" He pointed one black claw at Grandmother who had shrunk to her normal size when the fight began. "There can be no interference!"

"Not true." Her voice still seemed as loud, no matter her size. "You yourself can find allies to feed you power if you so choose, Vandelarius." Was that satisfaction in her voice?

He shrank back, fury vanishing, desperation taking over as his gaze flickered around the small group of demons huddled, watching. Not one of them seemed inclined to help him.

Aw. What a shame.

"Maybe if you weren't such an ass," I suggested, grinning. Couldn't help it. Really couldn't.

He snarled and attacked Dad again, but we knew now the party was over. His low blow could have taken Dad out if he'd been alone, a sneaky and underhanded shaft of fire aimed at Dad's more tender parts. But with us to reinforce his shields, leaving Dad his full power to fight back, the attack merely bounced off, returning to its sender, taking Vandelarius full in the crotch.

Even I winced, though I had no sympathy for him as he crumpled to the ground, hands covering what had to be a world of pain, his body shrinking slowly. Dad tromped forward, power pressing down on his rival, a massive hammer of magic, amber glow throwing sparks, hovering over his head. With a set and determined look on his face, Dad began to pound the other demon into the polished floor, as though he were driving home a particularly stubborn nail. By the time he was done, they were both normal sized and Vandelarius lay, curled on his side much as his son had been, eyes vacant, a string of drool trailing from his lip to the floor.

Someone was screaming, the same female demon I assumed

was Dad's sister. She rushed forward with a hiss, hitting him over and over again. Dad turned on her, toward us from his hunched position over the fallen demon, eyes glowing with power, a massive bellow erupting from his chest as he struck her, sending her flying.

Syd, help him. Sassy's power reached for Dad, Meira's too, mine surging a close third as we enveloped Dad in our love and held him tight while the power inside him, the primal power of a demon's draining, tried to turn him into a monster.

A long time ago, I'd told him it was my worst fear—that I didn't want to be a monster. He'd seemed surprised, hurt even. But looking at my Dad, the magic he'd taken from Vandelairus poisoning him with the need for more, I knew my worry had been well founded after all.

Knowing what he had just been through, though on a smaller scale, I let the girls out to help, certain it would take all of us to bring him back. It was weird, feeling them reach into him, almost leaving me they went so deep, the thrumming solidity of Shaylee's earth magic holding him still while my demon snapped and snarled against him, the vampire core of me filling him with spirit power. I wound him up in witch energy, the family magic welcoming him as it always had.

I was terrified it wouldn't work, to be honest. The beast in Dad's eyes didn't want to leave, fought us with the power of the Second Seat of Demonicon. But as strong as it was, it could never defeat so much love.

Dad came back to us, sagging as he panted, bending in half, body shaking from the effort. When he looked up, the animal inside him still flickered, but he was under control. I felt around inside myself then, with a touch of panic, and realized mine was still there too.

Good to know. At least I had an army of alternate personalities to keep me in check. Not so my dad.

He staggered to his feet, moving more smoothly by the time he was upright. His whole body shuddered, a ripple of amber magic running through him. Dad sighed, a deep gust of air from far within him before he strode forward and settled one hand on my shoulder and squeezing ever so gently.

Dad didn't say a word as he left us, striding with purpose toward Grandmother and the rest of the huddled family. His sister managed to pull herself together, blood trickling from her nose and mouth, glaring at him with absolute hatred even as she cradled Vandelarius's empty shell in her arms. He had a solid enemy there, but from the quivering fear rising from the rest of the gathering, she could hate him all she wanted.

Dad stopped next to the thrones, both intact despite the fact they'd broken his fall, facing Grandmother.

"Well done, my son," she said.

He glared at her for a long moment and I knew then the crossroads he'd reached. Sassy hissed at my feet, Meira pressing into my side as they both realized the same thing at the same moment.

Dad was going to challenge her. He was going to do it. Strip his own mother and take the Ruler's throne.

I wanted to reach out to him, to stop him. I loved him, he was my dad, but after what he'd been through, I wasn't sure we could save him the second time. And if he did it, if he took her power, I knew he'd never be the same again.

Grandmother smiled at him. She knew, too, clearly. But she didn't move or make an effort to convince him otherwise. Maybe it was what she wanted? I found that hard to believe. When she finally spoke, her tone was light, almost teasing.

"You make me proud, Haralthazar."

His body relaxed, the tension easing out of him, shoulders sagging just a little, head bowing and I sighed myself, a shaking exhale of air tasting of poison.

Dad turned then, away from her, and approached his throne, pausing only one more moment before taking his

Seat. He cried out, power rippling over him as the throne itself glowed with amber magic, sealing him to it, binding him to the plane and his place.

"Let nothing sever you from your duty," Grandmother said. "And when the day comes, may you Rule in my place."

"All hail!" Pagomaris rushed forward, throwing herself prone to the floor. "Prince Haralthazar, Heir to Ruler, Second Seat, Demon Prince of the First Plane."

34

It didn't take Grandmother long to make things even more official. Within an a few hours of the battle, the mess was cleaned up, the two empty demons carted off and Dad's coronation was underway with all the pomp and majesty the court could muster under the circumstances.

We had that short time with Dad, but it wasn't enough, not even close. Not when I again had the sense with every word he spoke he was telling us goodbye. No, he never came out and actually said it, but something about the sadness in him, the way he held my hand, the tone of his voice, made me think I didn't have a dad for much longer.

Probably just my overactive imagination.

It didn't take long for the demon aides to descend on him, for us to be chased off by Pagomaris, hurriedly dressed. I didn't fight her this time, let her drape me in some kind of massive feather thing with giant plumes sticking out of my head. I just didn't have the heart to fight anymore.

I'd had enough fighting for the day, thanks.

Two small thrones had been placed below Dad's, to my shock. The cold stone wasn't my first choice for a seat, but again I didn't argue when Meira and I were guided to them, Sassafras firmly in my lap.

This isn't usual, he informed us. *Ahbi isn't done playing.*

The coronation itself seemed to take forever as Dad strode up the concourse and bowed to Grandmother. He went through a series of oaths, up and down from his knees several times, had to drink three kinds of wine and eat three kinds of bread. A choir sang, their droning melody actually bringing tears to my eyes before he bent to accept a massive crown, weighed down with a robe crusted in jewels, a deadly looking scepter in his hands before he once again sat on his throne.

"Hathenemeira, Lady of the Seventh Plane, rise and come before us." Grandmother gestured to Meira who did as she was told, her own feather headdress bobbing over her. She actually looked kind of cool, like a showgirl or something.

Gave me hope I didn't look like a total idiot.

"You have fought bravely and acquired much power," Grandmother said. "Because of this, we now declare you Princess of the Second Plane."

Equals, huh? Meira was smiling, so I was happy for her. Not like we had much competition left, so she was safe enough. I had no doubt she could kick anyone's ass that came along.

Power surged to her from the thrones. Meira bowed and retreated.

"Sydlynhamitra, Princess of the Second Plane, rise and come before us."

My turn. I stood and set Sassy down, but he hopped off the stone seat and came with me as I stood before the Rulers, ignoring the family around me.

"Your prowess is unparalleled," Grandmother said. "Your power now without peer beyond the thrones themselves." Well that was shocking to hear. But as I thought about it, I agreed with her. Cypherion had been Vandelarius's heir after all.

Uh-oh.

"We declare you heir to Second Seat," she said while Dad scowled like a thundercloud and refused to look at me. "Future Ruler of Demonicon."

I didn't know whether to thank her with as much sarcasm as I could muster or keep quiet.

Quiet won.

Things wound down quickly after that. The family trooped off to the dining room two floors below while Grandmother rose from her throne, Dad next to her, and led us away. I followed, partly because I wanted to be with Dad and partly because I needed a chance to tell her where she could shove her status.

We sat near a window, Grandmother's power forming a bubble around us as the rest of the sycophants called "family", those that hovered and hoped for favor, were totally cut off.

Syd's making friends on every plane.

"I want to thank you, my girls," Grandmother said with warmth in her voice. "I've been waiting for a very long time for your father to finally come to his senses and challenge Vandelarius."

I scowled at her, temper clenched like a burning knot inside me. "Don't you dare," I snapped.

Even Meira looked pissed.

"Hear me out," Grandmother said. Sighed. Sat back as she looked out the window. "I grow old, dear ones. My life has been long and prosperous. But, unlike yours ever will, my very special granddaughter, the time of my passing finally draws nearer." She turned back, met my eyes even as Dad shifted beside her, grim, no longer full of rage, but acceptance. "Your father," she took his hand, squeezed it and he squeezed back, "is the best of my children, I've told you so."

"I never wanted this, Mother," Dad said.

"Which makes you the only choice for the throne." Grandmother's smile was the first real one I think I'd ever seen on her face, her expression open, eyes full of kindness. "I don't trust anyone else. That in itself, from an old politician, should be enough praise for you, my son."

Dad nodded, smiled a little back. "I know."

"Please, believe I had no choice." She seemed genuine. Stressing the *seemed*. "Things aren't as they appear here on our plane."

"The civil unrest?" I crossed my arms over my chest.

"You will make a fine Ruler someday," Grandmother said. "But yes. Uprisings are more common than ever, politics turning to murder with alarming frequency. The laws that have held us together all these millennia are contracting, falling apart. If we are to preserve our home, we must have strong leadership."

Dad grunted softly. "Maybe the old ways aren't the best any longer, Mother."

She looked like the very idea pained her, but she nodded. "I'm well aware," she said. "Which is why I need you so desperately, Haralthazar, and why now is the perfect time for your ascension."

His entire body relaxed and, for the first time, I saw Dad give in to what he'd become.

"We'll work this out together," he said.

"I know we will," Grandmother said. "And I will have you to carry on the legacy when I'm gone."

Sassafras's snort startled me. "Excuse me, Ruler," he said with great sarcasm, "before you go and get all weak and frail on us, I highly doubt you'll be stepping down any time soon."

Grandmother laughed, reaching out to scoop Sass into her arms, hugging him to her, hands stroking his fur.

"Impudent child," she said, eyes sparkling. "I still have a few centuries left." She let him settle in her lap. "But things must change slowly if they are to be accepted and Haralthazar needs time to establish himself."

I know I should have been a good girl and let my anger go. After all, the fate of Demonicon seemed to be at stake. But I was tired of the manipulation and political maneuverings.

"You can forget about me taking the Second Seat," I said. "Forget all of it. I'm going home, one way or another."

Grandmother nodded. "None of us are immune to the ways of our plane, Sydlynhamitra," she said. "Even I am a pawn in this endless game to keep our people safe. But you are correct in one thing. Your task is done for now. It might be best if the three of you," she smiled at Meira while handing Sassy back to me, "were to vanish until things settle down again."

Dad stared at her, face pale, hands clenched on the arms of his chair.

"Mother," he rumbled. "What have you done?"

She shook her head, gesturing as the veil parted before her, the cold, dim sight of the family basement clear on the other side.

I'd seen Dad angry, beside himself, in an animal-like rage fed by power. But I've never seen him so full of fury he couldn't speak.

Sassy did it for him.

"You trapped the girls here on purpose." He growled a soft whine, ears flat, tail thrashing against me. "Took their hope, forced them to fight. Ahbi, that's despicable, even for you."

I sat back, not really all that surprised, to be honest, as I met Dad's eyes. "Can you please tell me," I said, amazed at how light my tone was, "why you ever wanted to come back to this place?"

He shook his head, teeth grinding as he clearly fought the urge to do something unspeakable to his own mother. "You know," he said, "I really have no idea."

Dad surged to his feet, holding his hands out to us. "In fact," he said, "I think I'm about to change my mind." Meira took one of his hands as she rose, mine sliding over the warm skin of his palm as I joined her. "Well done, Mother.

But you've forgotten something." He pointed at the sight of the basement, the shimmering effigy winking back as someone turned on the single bulb over the pentagram. "I'm anchored to their plane. And I think it's time I went home. For good."

Grandmother stood, her face crumpling in weariness and pain. "Please, my son," she whispered it, the first time I saw her weakness. "I need you. Your world needs you. Do not abandon us again."

I felt Dad hesitate, the weight of his duty pulling him down.

"Dad," I said, squeezing his hand. "You're always welcome. You know that."

Why was he so sad? The fear of losing him forever came back. What was really going on here?

"Let's go." He pulled on my hand, leading me to the gap. I turned before he could push me through and met Grandmother's eyes.

"Thanks for the hospitality," I said. "And the life lessons. I won't be back."

Meira jerked free of Dad and lashed out at Grandmother with her power. "Neither will I," she snarled. "Happy now?"

She ran through the veil alone, but not before I saw the tears in my sister's eyes.

"You will return," Grandmother said, sadness pulling her face down. "You weren't the right choice, not yet, but someday you will sit next to your father, Sydlynhamitra. But I will see you before then. When I need you the most."

I refrained from giving her the finger while I worried she might be right and followed Meira home.

36

Gram was just releasing Meira as I stepped through into her wiry arms, forcefully pressed to her thin body while she shook and hugged me as if she'd never let me go. I clung to her just as hard, feeling the warmth of Sassafras as he wound himself around our feet.

I was jerked free of Gram's embrace and slammed bodily into Charlotte for half a second before she pushed me away from her and shook me so hard my teeth rattled together.

"Don't ever leave me again!" I had a moment to register she looked like hell before she hugged me again, hands clawed against my back. I let her feel my magic, slid it around her, held her with it until hands gripped her shoulders and gently pulled her free. Her long, blonde hair hung in limp strands around her face, cheeks and eyes sunken with dark circles, lips dry, flaking. She swiped at her face, tears pouring down her patchy skin, once flawless beauty now pasty and damaged.

Mom held her back, one arm around her as I continued

to feed the weregirl with my power. She stilled at last, her shaking, twitching body settling down, the color returning to two very bright points on her cheeks.

Charlotte slid free of Mom and squared her shoulders. "You're staying?"

I nodded. Reached for her. She swatted at my hands, the cold expression I was used to returning to her face though she continued to tremble just enough I knew she hid just how much harm I'd done.

"If you go anywhere," she snarled, "I'll kill you myself. Now, if you excuse me, I have to take a shower."

She stomped off as if I'd offended her, grumbling and muttering to herself, looking back over her shoulder at me several times before she disappeared up the stairs.

"She's been a handful." Mom hugged me, shaking herself, though she kept her tone light and soft. "How was your trip?"

I laughed into her hair, inhaling the scent of lilacs, amazed as I hugged her to look over her shoulder and see my very human hands.

"Oh, you know," I said. "Met the family."

Mom's deep laugh echoed mine. "How lovely."

Her blue eyes sparkled as she welcomed Meira, hugging us both.

It wasn't until she let us go and turned to face Dad that all the joy went out of her. I felt Gram's hand take mine, held it tight as Mom approached him.

"Harry." She reached out as if to touch him as his human form filled the effigy, grim expression telling her everything wasn't all right. "Thank you for bringing them home."

"Miriam." His voice caught as he swept her into his arms. A huge sob rose inside me, but why I didn't know. Damn it, this really felt like goodbye. "It's finally time."

Mom gasped, pulled away. "My love?"

"I didn't have a choice," he said. "I had to take the Seat."

Mom's whole body collapsed in on itself for a moment, but she pulled herself together before Dad could hold her up. "I see," she said.

"I don't." I pulled away from Gram and confronted the two of them, Meira right beside me. "Dad's been acting like this is the end of something ever since Grandmother made him fight." I looked back and forth between them, feeling my heart splinter as their eyes met, both of them so sad I knew what was coming.

"We have to sever our mating," Dad said, apologetic, broken.

No. No way. Not after everything we'd been through as a family—

"Now that I'm Second Seat," he told us, "I must take a demon wife. Have demon children. It's part of our law."

Mom let out a soft sound, tears on her face, but she didn't buckle, didn't waver again, looking as much like a statue as the one Dad inhabited.

I wasn't so solid. "This is all my fault." The sob finally came out, my chest aching from its release. "Mom, Dad. I'm so sorry."

But Dad was shaking his head, Mom too.

"Sweetheart," Mom said. "It's not." She sighed out some of her own sadness, the air heavy with it. "We both knew this day would come eventually." She smiled up at him, glittering tears making shining paths down her face. "Harry is immortal. I made him promise we would end our mating before I was too old."

"And with me so close to the Seat, we both knew it was coming." Dad kissed her softly. "I just wish we'd had more time. But I'm grateful for what we've had, my love." He met my eyes, then Meira's. "I want you both to know," his gaze drifted to Sassafras whose ears lay flat, body crouched low to the ground, eyes full of sorrow, "the three of you, without your help, I'd still be the monster I became when I emptied Vandelarius." I shuddered at the memory, felt the stirring of the beast inside me at the thought and nodded. "The lessons

I've learned here," he hugged Mom around the shoulders, "loving your mother, having you two, has taught me so much, so many things I can take back home with me. To make Demonicon a better place." He paused, swallowed a few times. And when he spoke again, his deep voice cracked. "Mating with Miriam, being your father, was the greatest thing I've ever done."

I rushed forward, hugged him, Mom pressed to my side, Meira between us, sobs clenched tightly in my chest as the truth of what he was saying finally broke through my denial.

When he finally let us go, his cheeks were wet, but he was smiling.

"I love you all so much," he said. "And I'm sorry things had to end this way. Syd, Meira, take care of your mother. And Miriam," he bent and kissed her gently, "my heart will never leave you."

Mom faked her best smile back but her face looked frozen, even as her lips quivered, hand clinging to his.

I turned away as Dad swept Mom into his arms and held her close, unable to watch their one last desperate, parting kiss. Meira wept on my shoulder before pulling back and facing them both with anger.

"This is *her* doing." I knew exactly who my sister was talking about. "And I actually thought I loved her."

Meira ran off, still crying, her footfalls pounding up the steps and overhead as she retreated to her room. Sassafras paused, bowed his head to Dad.

"Harry," he said, his own words full of grief. "Be well, my Prince." He then turned and scampered upstairs to comfort my sister.

Meira was so right. I stood there, cursing my grandmother, hating her with more passion than I'd ever felt as Mom and Dad finally separated. I slid my arms around Mom while Dad bowed his head. Ahbi—I would never call her Grandmother again—had finally done what so many others had tried to do, failed to do.

She'd destroyed our family at last.

Dad's hand rose, amber magic in a thread sliding out from his fingertips. Mom's own came up as if against her will, blue power flickering with green and white touching Dad's. I felt the power snap, saw their connection break, the recoil making Mom cry out while Dad's face crumpled.

He met my eyes as he left us, his statue again cold and shining, a diamond of incalculable value now worthless to me.

My dad was gone.

Mom wove a sheet of power, each thread connecting in

perfect harmony to the last until it was tangible, complete. With trembling hands but a resolute expression, she shook it out and up, draping Dad's statue in darkness.

37

I couldn't take it. Couldn't. I fled from Mom, from Gram, from all of it. Couldn't bear the touch of the veil, instead threw on my jacket and boots and felt the bite of the cold as I ran out into a frosty white world almost unfamiliar, across town, through the glass door, down the stairs, across the green barrier and into Liam's waiting arms.

The cavern's power embraced me, held me as close as my Sidhe friend as he guided me into his room and sat me on the edge of his bed. The draping branches of the carved tree above me drooped as though in tune with my sadness.

Liam held me, rocked me as I cried and babbled, unable to get anything out clearly for a long time. When I finally could, I'd calmed enough to pull away and stand, to pace, feeling odd as I did, my human body an adjustment after the muscular power of my demon form.

He listened as he always listened, face creased in concern, hands clasped in his lap, hazel eyes full of worry while I dumped the whole crappy, nasty, unfair situation on him, from the fighting to Dad's ascension and my new worry I'd never see my father again.

Galleytrot padded into the room part way through, keeping his head down, stretching out at Liam's feet as if he didn't want to interfere or intrude. But when I finally turned to them both, I crouched and hugged the big hound, feeling his power slide around me too even as his wet tongue stroked over my cheek.

"Syd," he rumbled a morning thunderstorm, "I'm so sorry."

Liam grasped my hands, pulled me into his lap. I sat there, tears welling again though I was sure the well of them was almost dry and cupped my face in his hands.

"You survived," he said, "more than that. You kicked ass. And your father… Harry will be okay, Syd. And I have absolutely no doubt you'll see him again."

"Mom just made it look so… final." I snuffled, wiping my nose on the cuff of my jacket.

Liam nodded sadly. "It probably feels that way to her," he said. "I can't imagine what she's going through." He slipped his arms around me, hugging me close. "But as long as your father's effigy is still here, you can see him. Right?"

I perked a little. Liam was totally right. And I was being an emotional freak.

As usual.

I lifted my head from his shoulder to smile at him, only to meet his lips. Liam kissed me gently, with a tentative touch from his warm lips, tension in his body as though he feared I'd reject him. For a long moment I didn't, hugging him around the neck, feeling the heat of his skin, the slow and welcoming pressure of his mouth on mine.

But I finally had to pull away. Stood up. Backed off, almost tripping over Galleytrot.

"Liam," I choked. "I didn't tell you everything."

He nodded a little. "I guessed as much," he said. Blushed. "I'm sorry I kissed you, but I knew you were going to tell me something I wasn't going to like and I didn't want to miss the chance."

Sweet. Adorable and sweet and lovely and just the very best person I'd ever, ever known. And here I was, about to break his kind heart, just like Galleytrot asked me not to.

"I can't be with you," I whispered. "Not ever. And not just you." I hugged myself, turned away from him, faced the hall and the distant view of the Gate in the far chamber. "I'm immortal. I'm going to live forever. Which means I can never be with anyone who isn't."

I suppose I shouldn't have been surprised to hear him laughing. I turned back, hesitant, really expecting to see despair on his face despite his good humor. Instead he smiled at me, eyes full of sparkle.

"At least it's not about Quaid." He stood up, came to my side, hugged me again, but without need behind it. Just a hug, an offering of support.

And I took it, no matter the consequences.

"Syd," Liam whispered into my hair as he held me, "it doesn't matter. It never will. Yeah, I only have a normal lifespan to look forward to with you. But I'll always love you, even if my ghost has to haunt you for eternity."

Great. Just what I needed, another echo to worry about.

"I can't even think about it," I said. "I'm sorry, Liam. But this changes everything."

The part of me that had considered saying yes to him, throwing my feelings for Quaid away and committing to what Liam had to offer, withered and crawled into an unhappy hole inside me.

"It does," he agreed. "I guess we'll just have to wait and see."

I loved him for his optimism, but sometimes it really sucked.

So much for a Merry Christmas.

Mom went from mournful to cold and brittle by the time I trudged my way home again, tears spent on the wide shoulders of the guy who loved me no matter what. I knew it was a defense mechanism of hers, but we needed her, damn it. I needed her. Still, I couldn't blame her for retreating into her Council Leader persona, abandoning her promise and diving into Council business to stay distracted.

Let's just say Christmas morning was a real downer and leave it at that.

It took me a few days to break Meira out of her angry shell. When I did, trapping her in her room with Sassafras for backup and letting her pummel me for a few minutes with her fists and her power—not telling anyone she broke the rules no matter what—she finally collapsed on her bed, sadness surfacing at last, and finally admitted to me the worst part of all of it was she felt like a traitor.

Despite what she told Ahbi, Meira wanted to go back to Demonicon someday.

Honestly, I was the last person to tell her how to feel, to reassure her she wasn't a bad person. Not when going back meant seeing Dad again.

Speaking of whom, we hadn't had a word from him and despite what Liam said I was starting to worry maybe he was gone from us forever too. The breaking of the thread between him and Mom—did that mean he could never come back? Yes, his effigy remained, but maybe it was their connection that held him.

I didn't have the heart to ask her.

Just wouldn't be fair.

Of course, I could always have just gone down to the basement and called him myself.

Sure. Just as soon as my heart put itself back together.

I did look in on it regularly, just in case. It hurt to see Sassafras curled up on Dad's feet pretty much every time I did. My demon cat was taking this as hard as the rest of us.

The thought of going back to school was so ridiculous I actually had a fight with Gram over it. She insisted I return to Harvard and I finally relented. Maybe absorbing myself in study would help me shake the deep melancholy holding the whole family in thrall. Even the coven was affected, power dim and sad as they mourned with us.

Charlotte seemed to recover quickly, though I caught her staring at me all the time and the first night I was home I found her sleeping in a nest of blankets at the foot of my bed when I stumbled over her on my way to the bathroom.

I didn't protest until the third night, gently steering her to her own room at last, knowing she had to break her fear of me disappearing somehow.

I tried to examine the bond she'd formed to me, but every time I reached for it I'd catch her glaring. After a few attempts, I dropped the effort and let her be. Her choice, her problem, though I hoped it wouldn't become a major issue for us one day.

The only one who seemed to be fine with the state of affairs was my demon. Not that she was pleased Dad was gone or anything, but her growth of power made her very, very happy. Funny, but I felt like I'd grown, too. No more poor me, this time.

About time, really.

The rebalancing of my powers did take my mind off things when I focused on figuring out what other changes my demon's new status meant. As long as Shaylee and my vampire were okay with it, so was I. When my demon started to puff up with her own importance, it was actually funny to feel the other two smack her.

Oh, the joys of being multi-me.

I tried several times over the first few days to reach Quaid, but he'd cut me off again. So be it. Not like I was in the market for a boyfriend anymore. This whole immortality thing hung over my head, feeling like finality, not infinity. And even though Liam still acted like nothing changed, that with enough time I'd soften, my sadness didn't go away. I could never be with Liam. No way was I doing that to the two of us. Dad and Mom's split was the icing on that particular cake.

Either I found someone as long-lived as I was going to be or I was on my own.

The second option had the most appeal.

In the last days before I left for school again, I found myself watching Gram a lot. This whole immortality thing was really dragging on me. Was she a little slower these days? Not quite so perky? Jokes not quite so quick on the draw?

I just couldn't go there. Not Gram. Not ever.

If only I could shake the nightmares waking me almost every night. The beast inside me laughing, roaring in triumph as she stripped first my father, then Ahbi, of all their power before ascending the Ruler's Seat.

Shudder.

Maybe I was a monster after all.

Like what you read? Find more at

pattilarsen.com

I grinned at the enthusiastic, if off key, rendition of *Happy Birthday* and added my own pathetically energetic voice. Twenty or so young witches, all about the same age as the birthday girl, sat around her as she gazed with wide, happy eyes at the candles on her impressive cake.

Mom might have been acting distant and a little cold the last six months, but she went all out for Meira's eleventh birthday. Guilt driven? Maybe. Still, I found it hard to stay mad at her no matter how little time she seemed to have for either of us these days.

My heart ached every time I thought of Dad.

No room for sadness today, though. Even Mom smiled and clapped her hands when the singing was over and Meira finally got to blow out her candles. The giant cake was covered in them, a model of our house back in Wilding Springs complete with a big black dog in the back yard for Galleytrot, a furry silver Persian in her window for Sassafras and the whole family of us in the front driveway. Well, not the whole family. We lived in a coven, after all. Mom, me—I refused to look too closely at my candy sculpture when the first glimpse I had made me think 'prostitute'— Gram and Meira. No Dad.

Ouch.

Despite his obvious absence, Meira squealed in delight over the monstrosity and it's many glowing candles, happily spinning little whirling balls of air to help her put them all out as she made her wish.

It would have been nice to host her birthday back home, in the real thing instead of standing next to its facsimile, but Meira was still in school. I'd been home over a month now, the spring semester over. Amazing how quickly I grew accustomed to my own bed again and how weird it felt to be back at Harvard, even if it was only for a few hours.

Mom's sitting room was as gloomy and dark as ever, but the giggling witches, balloons and animals shaped out of magic cavorting in the air over our heads made it feel much more festive. I swatted at a herd of unicorns galloping past my right ear, but couldn't help smiling.

Meira's friends piled in around her, handing her presents, holding out plates for their chunk of her cake. I hung back, not wanting to interfere, saving my gift for her for when she returned home tomorrow. Maybe it was silly for me to make the trip to Harvard for her birthday, but I hadn't missed one yet and didn't plan to start any time soon.

I was a little ashamed of the wave of jealousy I felt, seeing my little sister the center of what seemed like genuine affection and attention. I hadn't had access to other witches my age when I was growing up, partly because the age gap in births just happened to spread to older and younger than me for some odd reason, but also because of my sixteen years of rejecting my magic.

Yeah, my own fault. Still.

Lucky kid.

Mom met my eyes briefly over the laughing heads of the pack of eleven year olds, though her gaze dropped just as quickly. Erica hurried forward, taking over as Mom eased away. She'd run out of steam, I could only guess, and was getting ready to retreat.

I slid around the crowd, heading for Mom, just wanting a word, a moment, something to tell me the woman I loved still lived inside her. No matter what she said, I still blamed myself for the fact Dad was gone, his mating to Mom broken, now ascended to the Second Seat of Demonicon, one of its two Rulers. If I'd just listened to Mom and Gram, Dad wouldn't have to be Prince, take a demon wife, have demon children.

And Mom wouldn't avoid me like she was doing right now.

Did she hate me? The question crossed my mind many times in the dark of night over the last six months. I wouldn't blame her. I kind of hated myself, though I refused to let it show. The coven needed me to be strong for them. Even though Mom wasn't leader anymore, had no connection to our family magic-wise, they still felt the grief of Dad's loss, if only because he'd been a part of their lives as long as Mom and Dad had been mated.

I reached her just before she disappeared behind her office door, one hand on her arm. She turned to me, the barest of smiles remaining, the lines around her eyes and mouth deeper than I remembered. Losing Dad seemed to be aging her even more.

When did my mother start getting old?

"Syd," she whispered, kissing my cheek though her lips were dry and cold, her hands almost icy as they touched the sides of my face. "Take care of your sister."

I tried to pull her back, but she was gone already, in heart if not in body, then both as the door slid shut behind her. It was hard not to sigh and lean my forehead against her door, or to pound on it with both fists and tell her to wake up.

I did neither. Wouldn't do any good. Instead, I turned

back and faced the party, smiling at Meira whose amber gaze must have followed us as we retreated, sadness in her eyes.

Love you, Meems, I sent. *Happy birthday.*

I didn't last much longer than that. Once the cake was devoured and the presents torn open and admired, most of the kids left, picked up by their witch parents who treated me with a mix of deferential awe and fear. Well, I guess I was okay with that. Better than hate and revulsion.

Yup, I'd take it.

Erica hugged me as I stood from my chair, Meira huddled with three friends, giggling over something.

"How are you, Syd?" She stroked my cheek. Erica Plower had been Mom's second since I was little, and had always treated me like she was my mother too. She had new wrinkles too, though not as pronounced as Mom's. The old me would have brushed her off, anger rising. But my arms reacted without my consent and hugged her to me.

"I'm great, Erica," I whispered in her ear. "How are you?"

She pulled away after a moment, teary eyed but smiling, a real, happy smile. I think I surprised her. Surprised myself, actually. But ever since I'd come home from Demonicon I was hyper aware of the people around me, the ones I loved, cared about. How fragile they were.

Part of me wished Grandmother had never told me I was

immortal. But at least it made me more empathetic. And appreciative.

"I'm wonderful," she said, blonde hair back to its old bob, the one I missed. It swung around her face in shining gold strands and I found myself grinning at her.

She didn't get to say anything more. Meira burrowed her way between us and hugged me, her forehead pressed into my shoulder. She was getting so tall, and had matured so much in the last year, it was hard for me to remember she was only ten.

Wait. Eleven. Wow.

"Thanks for coming." Meira grinned up at me, cute black horns shining in the low light of the room, amber eyes lit from within. "I'll see you tomorrow?"

I nodded, hugged her again, pulling her tight before releasing her to go back to her friends. I waved at Erica, not prepared to go into any kind of deep conversation with her and headed for the elevator.

Charlotte stepped out of the shadows, my bodywere practically attached at my hip as I waited for the doors to open. She seemed to suffer no ill effects from my prolonged stay on Demonicon, despite the powerful reaction she'd had to my absence. I was happy to know she didn'f suffer any permanent damage thanks to my grandmother's arrogance. Still, Charlotte was very insistent she remain in close contact these days.

I found I didn't really mind it, though there were times it would have been nice to open the bathroom door and not find her waiting for me on the other side.

Guess I could get used to anything.

At least things had been quiet since we returned from Dad's plane. As Charlotte and I stepped out into the Yard and I reached for the veil, I felt a tiny shudder go through me at the memory of being trapped. Yes, that fear stayed with me, that somehow when I rode the veil one day Grandmother would be waiting to pull me over and keep me prisoner there forever.

Silly, maybe. And yet, I wouldn't put it past the old bat.

Powerful Ruler or not, she was a conniving politician without morals who used her family on a regular basis to get whatever she wanted. I'd take my human grandmother over her anytime.

As we stepped into the veil, the rubbery membrane that held the two planes apart, sliding through toward home, I thought of Gram with a twinge of worry. She'd been absent lately, wandering off on her own. Not that I worried about her, not in the least. Of anyone in our family, Gram had proven to me without a shadow of a doubt she was more than capable of taking care of herself.

No, I missed her, it was that simple. The air was warm on the other side of the veil as Charlotte and I stepped out into a secluded area of the park near the house, outside the reach of the family wards, neither of us missing a stride as we began the short walk home. Gram was my constant, even when she was still lost to us, spiraling in and out of madness. Now, back to her abnormal self and about as stable as she was ever going to get, her constant presence and her support in our co-leadership of the coven was something I counted on without question.

When she disappeared on me, I finally felt alone.

The sun was just setting as I walked through the back door. One feeling of the house told me Gram still wasn't home. A bit bummed and missing my family, I said an early good night to Charlotte and retreated to my bedroom, closing myself off a little.

No more poor me. I'd made that vow and I intended to keep it. But there were still times I just needed to be alone.

Good book in one hand and a half-bag of chips dug out from under my bed in the other and I was lost for a while.

One touch was all it took. I didn't hesitate, didn't think, just ran for the stairs, the back door.

The yard.

And him.

About the Author

Everything you need to know about me is in this one statement: I've wanted to be a writer since I was a little girl, and now I'm doing it. How cool is that, being able to follow your dream and make it reality? I've tried everything from university to college, graduating the second with a journalism diploma (I sucked at telling real stories), was in an all-girl improv troupe for five glorious years (if you've never tried it, I highly recommend making things up as you go along as often as possible). I've even been in a Celtic girl band (some of our stuff is on YouTube!) and was an independent film maker. My life has been one creative thing after another—all leading me here, to writing books for a living.

Now with multiple series in happy publication, I live on beautiful and magical Prince Edward Island (I know you've heard of *Anne of Green Gables*) with my very patient husband and six massive cats.

I love-love-love hearing from you! You can reach me (and I promise I'll message back) at **patti@pattilarsen.com**. And if you're eager for your next dose of Patti Larsen books (usually about one release a month) come join my mailing list! All the best up and coming, giveaways, contests and, of course, my observations on the world (aren't you just dying to know what I think about everything?) all in one place: **bit.ly/pattilarsenemail**

Last—but not least!—I hope you enjoyed what you read! Your happiness is my happiness. And I'd love to hear just what you thought. A review where you found this book would mean the world to me—reviews feed writers more than you will ever know. So, loved it (or not so much), your honest review would make my day. Thank you!